# Wicked Fortune

REBECCA BAKER

Copyright © 2024 by Rebecca Baker

All rights reserved.

No portion of this book may be reproduced in any form without written permission from the publisher or author, except as permitted by U.S. copyright law.

***

Sign up for my newsletter and receive a free romance novel:

https://sendfox.com/rebeccabaker

# Chapter One

## MAGNUS

Bushwick, Brooklyn. A mishmash of gentrification, eyesores and warehouses, and ghetto.

I lean back in the leather chair in my Battery Park office. It's away from the flash and glitter of other parts of Manhattan, which suits me fine.

I don't give a fuck about that. Just like I don't give a fuck about the letter in front of me, hand delivered by Jenson, my father's attorney. Talk about posthumous posturing from the old man.

Still...

I've been waiting for this envelope with its thick cream paper, my name handwritten in strong penmanship, ever since my brother Hudson got his letter. And then got his inheritance. The woman he married is pretty and unexpectedly perfect for him. But that life doesn't interest me.

Fucking who I want to fuck, and when I want to, suits me down to the ground. And money. I like money. I have more than enough of that—my inheritance and the billions I've earned. However, my own fortune made by my hands and my very unerring ambition to rule the real estate development world in this cutthroat city is what pumps my blood and drives me. No tease from a dead man about trinkets supposedly lost to the past and legend will take me from my path.

I'm making my own fortune my way. I'm making my own mark on the landscape and my plans are big. There's no room for a dead man's last gasp for control from beyond the grave.

Look at what my brother needed to do.

Hudson had to find love, and he claims he found it with Scarlett, his bride. Jesus, they've only known each other a few months and I can't think of anything worse than being shackled to some woman for the rest of your life. Or ever.

We were brought up on tales of our inheritance. Not the monetary one, but the legend of jewels that have been nothing more than rumor my entire life. And they can stay that way. Sinclair real estate, what the family money was built on, is just fine and it can keep being fine. I've shares, we all do, but I'm no lackey. I don't jump when told to and I don't give a shit about sparkling jewels or getting fucking married.

I have bigger, better fish to fry.

Like my Bushwick project.

Pushing the letter to one side, I stare at the plans in front of me.

One ugly block in Bushwick I'm buying for a steal.

It's my biggest project, my most ambitious.

This baby is my real vision, what I've been working toward for years, and something new. Not only housing, but a whole living, breathing city of its own. A city within a city, if you will.

It's going to put me on the map as the biggest developer on the Eastern seaboard. My billions mean nothing without the power, the clout. Without carving my own name into the skin of New York.

This one ugly block is key. The location is perfection. Far enough from Manhattan and the enclaves of affluent Brooklyn. The block is close to transportation, and once it blooms, the entire area which I've been buying up will have people clawing to get their hands on the surrounds as well as a piece of history in the making.

The whole area will change. And I'll be behind it all.

My fortune will skyrocket. My name synonymous with the future of real estate development.

I'm taking the eyesore block and turning it into a luxury oasis of a city. A place with high end dwellings, offices, stores. Private parks that rise into the sky. Leisure centers and community spaces. Open air spots and closed areas for relaxation, community, play. It will be both new and familiar, and the type of place that will change the flesh of Brooklyn forever.

This is stage one. The most important. In the future that I've carefully orchestrated—a ten year ambitious plan—I have two others planned here, three more in Queens, and then I'll be hitting the Bronx. All of them are designed to fit the landscapes of the areas, and all will change them. My vision will bring me more fortune and power than I ever thought I could have before I embarked on this path.

Beyond New York? That's in my head, too.

But Bushwick...

This one block is going to be the flagship of my new empire.

Everything is ready to begin.

Only one thing stands in my way of buying out and driving out the riff raff.

One small thing.

It's not the Sinclair jewels, although I'm sure my piece that sits on offer comes with its own manufactured challenge from my dead father.

No. It's something else.

Five foot two, maybe three. Female.

Inconsequential.

And yet this creature is proving more difficult to squash than I thought.

Zoey Smith.

I shouldn't even know her fucking name.

She's a hold out on the block. The tiny but strong roadblock I need to eliminate before I can begin.

But everyone has a price and her tiny hole-in-the-wall store can't hold up against me or my money. Someone is sweetening the offer right this very minute. The amount on offer, the bells and whistles it comes with, is beyond what her place is worth, but getting her out of my way is worth it. Only a fool would reject my offer. And money always wins. It's only a matter of time.

And that time is now. She'll sign tonight, and I'll hit the ground running tomorrow.

I'm not worried at all.

Someone knocks on the door. I look up. My mother stands there. Tall, glamorous, and impeccably dressed. I grit my teeth as she approaches across the white-washed wooden floor and comes up to my marble and steel desk in a flurry of expensive perfume.

"Magnus—"

"Now's not the time, Mother." I flick a glance at her, a suspicious one. I love her, but with the letter appearing, I don't trust her. I know exactly where I get my devious streak from, and she's in my office right now.

"I'm your mother. Make time."

"Time's money and I'm working."

"You're always working, Magnus."

I raise a brow. "There's always work to be done and money to be made. And I'm in the middle of something huge."

"As always."

I want to be annoyed by that, but it's true. So I just fold my arms and wait. The woman's here for something and I've a pretty good idea what it is.

She frowns as she rests a hip against my desk, one long, tastefully painted fingernail tapping on the letter. "You're as driven as him."

"My father?" I laugh softly and shake my head. "Don't compare us."

The sigh is soft, loaded with disappointment. "You just got the letter. The Sinclair jewels are—"

"I'm not the one who cares about them. And I haven't, ever. That would be Ryder. He can have mine."

"Magnus."

I raise a hand. "Jewels are jewels, Mother. Pretty, but useless and a terrible investment."

"It's not always about money, Magnus," she says quietly, looking up past me to the huge wall of windows where we can see the river and Brooklyn beyond. "This is about family."

Part of me wants to say fuck family, but I don't. "Don't tell me my brothers have sent you in to convince me to get married. Hudson's gone and done that. I'm not interested."

"Did you read it?"

"Someone else can have my share. Again, Ryder," I say. "We're billionaires, and the jewels are pointless baubles."

She shakes her head and picks up the unopened envelope. "Not pointless. History. Your history. Read the letter, Magnus. Selfish doesn't suit you."

"Me not wanting to be a part of this crap isn't selfish."

"It is when it affects your brothers." She hesitates, then says, "I shouldn't have to tell you this, but the Sinclair family business is important to your brothers."

I sigh, aware she's trying to manipulate me. "Hudson told me the terms, Ma." She winces at the term. "But I'm not playing."

"To keep the family business is more than money, Edward Magnus Sinclair."

My full fucking name. She likes to play hardball. Anyone who thought my father was the tough one didn't know this woman. "What's it to you, Faye?"

Her eyes narrow. "I remained close to your father after the divorce, and you're my child. It matters. To lose your heritage...do you want that?"

Me? I'm building my own, but I do love my brothers, and I know what this means to them. Well, Ryder and Hudson. Even, I guess, Kingston, although with him, it's about the monetary value and what the family name brings. Still, I know what the woman is doing. "I'm not into manipulation, and I'm not getting married to suit some bizarre whim of a dead man."

My mother opens the letter and smooths it out. "There's a twelve-month period. And today is the start of your four weeks to fulfill your part. If you don't, then all of you lose your claim over the family business. Out of private and into public hands. It will be lost forever."

Fuck. I don't want to be the one who is the catalyst for that. But I don't say anything, because I know she's not finished.

"Magnus, to get your piece of the Sinclair jewels, the earrings—"

"They don't go with my aesthetic."

She ignores me. "You're headstrong, driven, more than your brothers. You never seem to care about anything apart from your goals and bottom line, Magnus."

"You say that like it's a bad thing." I swing my feet on my desk, tapping my fingers against my thigh. I almost say at least I'm not a cynic like Kingston, but

I doubt she'd see the difference between ambition and cynicism. "Fine. I'll get to it when I have a chance."

My mother's lips press together and the look she gives me makes me feel about five. "This isn't about marrying for love like Hudson. This is proving there's more than the hardness. More than building your fortune, which, if you ask me—"

"I don't."

"—you have more than enough of."

"Noted," I say.

"You need to prove you have heart."

"So I'll donate money. Put up a plaque. Adopt a fucking puppy."

Her eyes harden at my language.

"A three-legged puppy with a sad history."

Now her eyes narrow. "It's more than that. You need to prove you *care*, Hudson, truly care, about something more than money. And you have four weeks. From your birthday."

"Yeah, well—"

"That's today."

I give her a startled look. And almost laugh. I don't know why I forgot. That's why my brothers called earlier. I haven't had time to call them back. I wouldn't have taken my mother's call, and she knows it, so that's why she's here in person. "Birthdays are for children."

"Everyone, dear," she says, her mouth quirking a little, even though the worried light remains in her eyes, dark like mine. "Not even your ruthless attitude can stop the years passing. Do this. And remember, you'll need to prove you've changed."

She stands and places the letter on the desk, then reaches into her bag and pulls out a small package. "Happy birthday."

She leaves and I glower down at the letter. Yeah, happy fucking birthday to me.

I'll deal with this shit later. Instead, I push the letter and the wrapped package to one side and drop my feet back to the floor. Then I grab my phone.

I need to deal with this Zoey Smith situation first, and then I'll deal with the inheritance bullshit.

Proving I have heart. What a crock.

Still…it's not a hard one.

Showing heart should be easy enough to fake.

Maybe I'll kill the two birds with one perfect stone.

"Strippers?"

I glare at my grinning brother, Ryder, as he leans back in his chair in the upscale lounge deep in TiBeCa. This is totally his vibe; hot women abound. And with the photographers outside, I'm sure there's someone stupidly famous here tonight. We're just loaded.

But places like this make him happy and as long as there's booze and company I actually like being around, I don't mind it. Personally, I'd rather spend the night working, but I'm waiting on the call that my problem has taken the offer, so… here I am.

Hudson is there with his new wife, looking happier than I've ever seen him. They did a rush job marriage because she didn't want some big affair and neither did he. Let our mother get her hands on something like a wedding and we're talking months of prep and full-blown headaches.

But the Sinclair ring is on Scarlett's finger. He's all smiles and they're in the fairy tale stage, the one I've seen friends go through—our father go through—until the shine wears off and everyone wants to get out of the marriage contract and constraints.

Except… they don't have that look. They look blissed out. It's sort of disgusting. I shoot Ryder a look. "No strippers, what's wrong with you?"

"I'm thinking of you."

"It's tacky."

"I'm just a philanthropist. I'm into supporting different industries. Especially female centric ones."

I hide my smile as I take a swallow of my tequila. "You're thinking of yourself and your dick, Ry."

"My dick is very important. It has needs. Women love it and I love to give, as you know. But I'm talking strippers, not hookers. My dick's not involved."

"Fuck, you have issues."

"I'm supporting female industry," he says, taking a swallow of his drink and crossing his legs. "I like to watch. And I thought you might like to see a show."

I raise a brow. "Do I look like I enjoy that kind of thing?"

"Yes. Unless you changed teams when I wasn't looking. There are some all male shows. I'm willing to indulge your—"

"Idiot."

A hot blonde makes eyes at Ryder and he doesn't move, only smiles and she starts slinking over. I'm pretty fucking sure he'll be getting his own private strip show shortly.

A hand comes down on my shoulder. "I hear you caved."

I flick a glance up at my other brother, Kingston, who's just arrived. He's in a three piece suit, so whatever events went on in his business life today probably involved something important.

"Not caved, but the family business is on the table."

Kingston sips his Scotch and takes a seat next to me. "Our father was always a manipulative bastard. We should just sell it."

"And crush Ryder's dreams of getting his hands on a piece of family history? No, I can do this. It'll be easy. All I have to do is show I have heart. I'll set up some charities, maybe swoop in and save some struggling company. I have it under control."

I look at King. "You want to sell?"

"The family business is our heritage, but it's a money maker, so not particularly. I just don't like manipulation."

"Me either. But this is nothing at all."

Just then my phone starts to ring and I excuse myself, handing my drink to my brother and I weave through the crowd until I hit the pavement outside. I'm only having birthday drinks because Scarlett's soft hearted and organized it with Ryder, who is always up for a good time.

I hit answer. "Yeah?"

"We got a problem, boss."

Georgio doesn't even have to say what it is. I already know. Five foot almost nothing of a problem. "What happened?"

"We got the last signature, as you know. It's just this fucking girl. She owns her building. She's struggling to make payments, but we can't price her out. I've tried underhanded, I've tried bullying. I've tried to scare her with some muscle. I even offered her that sweet deal tonight."

"Let me guess." I lean my head back against the brick wall as the beat of the music from within cuts through the chatter around me. "She turned you down."

"We can go for more money. Add some other things. I wanted to check with you first."

I'm about to green light it, but I stop. Who the fuck does this girl think she is? She can't afford to turn me down, so there's more here, and it's going to take a little work to find out what that is.

"No. She's already been offered millions. This needs a different approach."

"I'm ready, boss," says Georgio. "Whatever you think."

Thing is, every problem has a root cause, and that leads to the solution. I need to do this myself. This is something that requires a deft touch, possibly underhanded. I really don't care. I just want the right results.

"I'll handle this one, leave it to me."

When I hang up, I close my eyes.

Everyone has a price. It's the matter of finding it. The thing that makes them tick. A plan starts to form.

Everyone has a weak spot. A breaking point. A thing they can't resist. Whatever the fuck you want to call it. Everyone has one.

I'm going to find this Zoey Smith's price and weak spot. I'm going to find the thing she can't resist.

And if I have to destroy her to do it, so be it.

It's dark, raining, the following early morning. I look at the narrow, dusty little store on the ugly street.

From across the street, the traffic sprays up filthy water as the rain pounds down. I'm relatively dry under my umbrella.

The store is nothing. It's shabby. A narrow piece of history that should have met the wrecker's ball decades ago.

A light shines from beyond the dingy window proclaiming *Through the Cover of a Book*. Underneath, in peeling cursive script, the paint reads *Magic Awaits*.

I mull it over.

Others just say secondhand books. Or name it after themselves or their gran or their three-legged sad puppy. This one promises the whimsical. It promises dreams.

Zoey Smith, I'm thinking, is a dreamer. The store isn't just a business front. I don't believe she's that savvy to ride on a book lover's weak spots, although maybe she is. But I'll be surprised. No, everything I'm looking at says dreamer. Someone who loves books. Someone for whom money isn't front and center.

In short, an idiot.

If I walk in with my umbrella and try to sweet talk her, or reason, it's not going to work. I recalibrate my plan a little. It's a good one, but a little fine tuning is always a boon. It's how I get ahead. I pay attention to details.

No one here knows who I am. I don't have a need to come down here. More so, I have everything under Edward Sinclair, my legal name. I don't like Edward, but it suits me to use that. Just like staying away from the limelight does. I leave that splashy bullshit to Ryder.

So she wouldn't have heard of Magnus Sinclair. Or Magnus Simpson, as I'm going with.

The problem with Zoey Smith, who on paper is a nothing, a thorn of stubbornness in my side, is that others might follow suit if I let her win.

She's not going to win. The woman sells books and cookies and cakes. Which is so downhome crap I can't believe she's lasted this long in this part of Bushwick. She's not in hipster heaven central. She's in the ghetto, basically.

I'm still working on the baked goods angle. She sells them and I'm not sure how legal that is. I let it slide, confident she'd crumble long before. But I make a note to up the ante on that front. On all the fronts.

And as for the Sinclair fucking game my dead father's playing, I'm setting up some charities. Heart. I have one. It's in my chest. Pumping blood. The sentimental interpretation is utter bullshit, but yeah, I'll play for my brothers. And even for me, I suppose. The legacy looks good. It helps with my clout. And though I don't need help with that, there'll come a time when I might, so I'm interested in building all my blocks, strengthening everything I can.

There's a small sign that's been in her window for ages, according to my people. For a job. They've scared off all potentials, stolen the ones that have promise. I figured if she couldn't find someone to fill her sign for a position offered, then it would weaken her. So far it hasn't.

But now… now it's perfect.

I'm going to apply.

And undermine her from within.

But I need the right approach. Whimsical name of her store. Cookies and other crap on offer along with the old books. I'll bet she's one of those people with a perpetually bleeding heart.

I'm not going in dry. Literally.

I collapse the umbrella and I give it to a woman hurrying by. She's soaked, but after a quick, suspicious look, she takes the umbrella and I stand there, letting the water soak into me. Pushing my now wet hair from my face, I open the folder I have with my fake resume and I let it get soaked. Then I fold it and slide it into my jean's pocket.

Bedraggled, harried, in need of a job. That's me. Or the me Zoey's going to meet.

If I'm right, she's going to give me the job without seeing the resume.

I take a beat to get myself into my new role, and then cross the street, dodging traffic. Outside, I take a breath and then I push open the door and step inside.

I drip on the floor in the cool and fairly quiet air. Just the traffic from beyond and the low strains of some classical piano fill the empty air. There's no one here. I frown, looking around, and from the back someone emerges.

A woman. Small, compact, with curling black hair stands there behind the counter. Her face bursts into a sunny smile.

"I'm Magnus Simpson," I say. "I'm here about the job?"

# Chapter Two

## ZOEY

Relief. That's relief I feel that someone's actually asking about the job.

They haven't in a while. And I'm sure if there wasn't pressure from the evil empire, aka EMS Group, the billion-dollar development company that are bullies in suits, I'd have found someone by now.

Yes, that rush of blood that washes through me is that, and nothing to do with the drop dead gorgeous man standing there.

He's tall and lean, with dark hair and onyx eyes, and beneath the T-shirt is a killer body. I know that because he's soaked; the shirt sticking to him, his wet hoodie draped over one strong arm. The worn but clean jeans and boots on his feet compliment the look. I almost want to pinch myself to see if I'm dreaming.

It if were me, I'd look like some kind of bedraggled subway rat. This man? Oooh, boy, he's like some pin up supermodel god from the ocean.

As the water drips down a thick strand of black hair and trails his face, the sheen of the rain brings focus to those high cheekbones, a freshness to his beautiful, sensuous mouth. And those eyelashes. I need a fan. Possibly smelling salts. Therapy for my pheromones and punch drunk hormones.

Someone print a label and slap illegal on this man.

Of course, there's also that possibility I'm dreaming. I might be. Last night I barely slept with worry and the latest onslaught from the Sinclair corporation. The name is all over the place and in the fine print of the contracts given to other businesses who've been priced out or sold out.

Not me. Those bullies can scrape my dead body from this spot. And if they do, I'm going to come back and haunt them.

The man—Magnus he said his name was—isn't the usual for the area. He's a little too well dressed. Even soaked to the bone, I can see that. He's white, and looks like he should be in one of the gentrified areas, maybe Williamsburg or Park Slope. He's not hood or working class. I'm not judging... okay, I'm totally judging, but I grew up here, and he doesn't have the look.

Then again, the man hasn't got an umbrella and he's looking for a job in a rundown barely above water secondhand bookstore, so what do I know?

But he's not the usual fare for this place. At all.

A few blocks east and it's hipster enclave Bushwick, but here? It's one of the small hole in the wall places where people work to make ends meet. There are a few gangs and projects and warehouses around. It's no frills, this place, and bodegas dot the landscape, not the fancy ass twenty-four-hour fresh juice and kale delis. The ones here sell lotto tickets, cigarettes, cans of 40s malt liquor, baseline groceries in cans, and Wise brand salted snacks.

In short, this Magnus doesn't look like someone who needs a job in a secondhand bookshop in Brooklyn.

Then again, never judge a sexy book by its sexy cover, and this man is one sexy cover of a book. I swallow. I'm off track again. I plaster on a smile. "Do you want a towel?"

"Just a job." His face creases with concern and my heart clenches. "Unless it's already gone."

"The job? My job?"

"Yeah, you know, the sign in the window? Thought I'd apply." He smiles at me and there's a hint of a dimple in his left cheek that's utterly swoon worthy.

I suck in a lungful of the coffee and sugar laced air with the hint of leather and spice that always seems to come from old books. I decide to check, just to make sure. "The sign's for here. This place. You're looking for a job? Here?"

I sound like a complete idiot.

He raises a brow and looks around. I just opened and no one is here yet. It's a bookstore. People don't normally come in for books until later. Or at all. Which is why I've got the baked goods and coffee. People need those.

"This is a small secondhand bookstore," I say, just to make sure. "Maybe you got off the wrong stop on the L."

"Nope. I live a few blocks away. I walked."

It makes sense. He's come in the wrong direction. He must be a hipster.

But then he names a street that's definitely not in the hipsterverse.

"Is the job still available? I saw the sign the other day, and it's still here, so I was hoping to apply." He looks about. "I don't see anyone else, unless there's a horde of invisible people lining up."

I laugh, I can't help it, and I wipe my suddenly sweaty palms against my jeans. He can't work here. I'll get arrested for unsolicited ogling or something. "I'm sorry, you just don't look like someone who usually goes looking for a job." That's a slight exaggeration, as when someone does venture in, there are all kinds. Not that anyone's been in for a while. Or when they have, actually returned.

I scrub a hand over my mess of frizzy hair. "I'm sorry, it's early and I was up late baking. I'm being a bad host." Now he's looking at me like I'm from outer space. "Would you like some coffee or a cookie?"

He frowns and for a moment there's a hardness to him, but it must be the early morning light coming in through the store front window. "Is that normal for a job interview?"

Is it? "I don't know," I say. "I've had that sign up forever."

His face falls and he shifts his feet on floor. "So you're not looking to hire?"

"Yes. I mean...I can't pay much—"

"Neighborhood prices rising? It's why I moved out here. Can't afford Manhattan. Not since..." He looks away, sliding his hands in his pockets, which brings my attention to those narrow hips and— I drag my gaze firmly up. "Not since I lost my job a few months ago."

A rush of sympathy runs over me and I usher him over to the counter. I hop behind it. Though he never answered, I put a chocolate chip cookie on a small plate and thrust it at him, and then I set the espresso maker for two cups, not one. There's milk and sugar already out. "Did you work in a store?"

"Marketing, actually, but I was ready to move on, and..." He casts an eye over the crooked aisles of books that spread out from the center of the store. "You don't need my life story."

I grab my cookie slash breakfast from the desk where it's been sitting as I've set up for the morning. The subway isn't far from here, only half a block, and I usually get people coming in for their morning commute.

"Not to sound desperate," he says, and his voice is low and soft and beguiling as he toys with the cookie on the plate I shoved at him, "but any money will be helpful."

"It's part time. I'm trying to stay afloat."

"Rent," he nods wisely.

"No, I own the building. It's been in my family for a long time, but utilities and taxes are a bitch, and with the development company wanting to buy all and sundry and turn this into a store-bought cookie block, it's getting harder."

I blink, and take a bite of my cookie to stop myself chasing him off.

"I'll take anything. It'll really help."

Truth is, I can't exactly afford it, but running this place by myself seven days a week is something I also can't afford. I need time to bake. I need time to scour for new stock. I need to set traps for the goons the billionaire uses to try and chase me from my home and business.

The aroma of roasted coffee fills the air and I place a cup on the counter in front of him and load mine with lots of sugar. Sweet and strong, and a splash of milk. I lean on the counter and look up at him.

Magnus doesn't put anything into his, just sets down the cookie and picks up the cup and takes a sip. "Thanks. There's a lot of closed businesses here."

"I know. EMS—that's part of the vile Sinclair billionaire real estate family to you and me—is hell bent on buying the whole place up and turning it into something boring."

He shrugs. "You could make a pretty penny."

"There's more to the world than raking in money." I finish my espresso and take a violent bite of my cookie. "And this part of Bushwick has character."

"That's one way of putting it," he says. His soft smile takes the potential edge from his words.

I lean against the counter and look up at the ornate ceiling. Each floor has the same intricate ceiling, back from when detail mattered and beauty ruled over the mighty dollar. "This place's part hasn't been sullied by gentrification's filthy hand." Breathing out, I tell myself to get a grip. "I'm into mixing it up, that's part of Brooklyn—the changing neighborhoods. But pricing the poorer people, the working class out creates problems and... I'm about to launch into a speech." I grin. "But yes, there's a job."

"So this development company hasn't tried to get you to sell?"

"Yes." I take another vicious bite of the cookie. "They have."

"So the job's only short term."

"Oh, I'm not going anywhere. I refuse. This is my place, and I've poured my entire life into it. I love the neighborhood and the books and I'm not selling. No goon is going to stop me." I lean onto the counter a little further, as a small drop of water clings to that lock of hair on his forehead. "I'll tell you this, though, if I don't sell, then the whole thing's going to fall apart."

"I like your passion...?"

Heat floods me. "Zoey," I say, holding out a hand, happy not to talk about the mess I'm in. "Zoey Smith, of the unknown Brooklyn Smith family."

"Magnus Simpson," he murmurs. "Nice to meet you, Zoey Smith of the Brooklyn Smiths."

And his big, strong hand closes about mine.

For a moment I can't think.

It's a buzz of sweet electricity, this touch and it jolts me down to my toes. "Nice to meet you, Magnus. As I said, there's a job, and it's not for a week or two until I sell. I'm not selling. And if I don't, others will back out. So."

I smile brightly because damn, his touch fills me with a glow that feeds my blood.

"I need someone to help me out. Making it work with just me is hard. I can do it, but I'd really appreciate the help. It's a regular old job. No brain surgery required.

"Ring up sales, make sure the coffee and baked goods are stocked, keep an eye on the upstairs. Help customers out. Most people know what they want. Some come in mainly to meander, like Tuesday Harry. He occasionally buys some books, but just prefers to mostly haunt the aisles, and I always give him a cookie or a muffin or a slice of cake and a coffee. His wife died last year and coming here gives him something to do. I don't know where he'll be going now, once his building's sale is complete. And—"

Oh, God. I'm writing him tomes of things he doesn't need. I glance down as I try to get what's left of my brain together. Double oh, God. I'm still shaking his hand. I'm clinging to it like a lifeline. And I don't want to let go.

I do. I'm not that crazy.

I catch a whiff of dark citrus laden with the subtle midnight scents of whiskey. Sweet and erotic and rich.

With a breath, I let go of his hand and take a step back.

But the man doesn't run. He doesn't even cast a furtive glance to the door. He's still wet and it's still pounding down rain out there, but he just smiles, looking about thoughtfully as he nods to himself. Then his onyx gaze rests on me and another jolt of warm electricity rushes through my bones, and my stomach dances the Charleston a moment.

"Maybe we could introduce your Harry to my gran," he says, bending his head down a little to me, his voice low. "When she's better."

My heart squeezes and I wonder if his gran is why a man like him is looking for a part-time job. Maybe he looks after her? I don't realize I've said that aloud until he laughs.

"I'm helping her out. She's a wonderful woman. Gave up everything for me to get me ahead in life, give me a chance. So I want to give back in her time of need."

"Is... is she sick?"

Magnus is quiet for a while and I've a horrible feeling I overstepped, but then he offers a small smile that breaks my heart.

"She's old. She had a fall and she's a stubborn lady who doesn't want to be a burden. She isn't at all, but that's my gran. The greatest lady you could meet. So yeah, a job, any job that lets me spend time with her and help her out will help me."

"I understand." I look up at him. "I think you might be a good man, Magnus."

"I don't know about that."

"I do. You're a good person. I can tell." I nod sagely. Damn, this man is tall. I go to say more when the bell on my front door rings and a teen with baggy jeans and a ball cap with a flat bill comes in.

He pulls off the wet oversize hoodie he has on and does an exaggerated air punch like he's some kind of MMA fighter, his little signature move. The kid loves mixed martial arts.

"Yo, Mama S, how you doin'?"

The kid has attitude, but he's sweet. "Hi Mikey."

He stops and slides a long, suspicious look at Magnus. "You want me to take care of this?"

"He's interviewing for the job," I say.

He's about a foot shorter than Magnus, but Mikey puffs up and lays on the machismo. "Yo, dude, you mess wit' her, you mess with my peeps, you hear me?"

I groan but Magnus nods, his face unsmiling, although I can see the glimmer of humor in his eyes. Mikey's about fifteen and I've known him since he was little. He's smart though, and I'm getting him into books, helping him find what he likes.

I pop two cookies in a bag and twist it shut and then slide it across the counter.

Mikey glances about, head bobbing, and like he's doing some kind of drug deal, then snakes the bag off the counter and into the pack on his back. He gives Magnus another suspicious look and sidles up to me.

"Zoey, I'm liking that book you gave me."

"I have another one, if you're interested." I say this like it's no big deal. "When you're done with the current one."

His face lights up, and then he shrugs with exaggerated nonchalance. "Yeah, maybe. See ya around."

He slouches out of the store and I start heading back behind the counter to put the rest of the cookies on display when Magnus speaks.

"That isn't good business."

"What isn't?"

"Giving shit away." He pauses, "to punks."

"Mikey's a good kid."

Magnus looks like he wants to say something, but instead he shrugs. "Not my place. It's just you said things were hard. If I do get the job, I'd like to know the rules."

"He's reading and a cookie here and there doesn't break the bank."

"Why do I suspect you give them away more than you let on?"

"I bake them. Anyway, my store," I say, "my rules."

"So it is." He sighs. "Did I ruin my chances?"

My heart lurches. "No, not at all."

"Great. When can I start?"

I blink rapidly, trying to get my brain into gear. "Tomorrow? How is tomorrow?"

"Tomorrow," he says, smiling at me, wooing me with that hint of a dimple. "Is perfect. I'll see you then."

And it's not until he's out the door that I realize a few things.

One, I never told him how many hours I'd need him.

Two, I never told him how much I'm able to pay an hour.

Three, I don't have any employee details.

Four, he never gave me a resume.

I slump down against the counter. Chances are, he was nothing more than the figment of a lonely imagination. Not that I'm lonely, but it's been a while, so my imagination is definitely lonely. And if he *is* real, he probably won't be back.

Still, I can't worry about that until tomorrow. Because I've a whole day to face, and, as the bell dings behind me, that includes a pile of bills and warding off the vile evil Sinclair empire.

I can't wait.

# Chapter Three

## MAGNUS

Jesus fucking Christ, that woman is something. Bleeding heart, soft as marshmallow, a total pushover. She didn't even ask for a resume. She gave me some sugar-laden treat, and a coffee.

How the hell my people didn't get her to sign the building the moment they met her is a mystery. I need to spend a few days with her at the least, to see the best way to get her to sign it over.

Fuck me offering her buckets of money.

She can pay market price. That's the punishment for getting me hands on level involved in this. I'm going to have to spend time with her. And all her sugar. By that, I don't mean those cookies and whatever the fuck else she bakes. No, I'm talking *her*.

Zoey Smith also has a stubborn streak fueled by a Do the Right Thing vibe.

I can get her. I know it. It's just going to take a while. I tap my pen against the pad on my desk as I stare out at the night line of Manhattan.

Okay, I'll give her a little more when she finally signs, on account she's so fucking naïve it actually hurts my black heart. The building is worth less than what it was bought for. I'm not sure how up to code it is, either. And her selling food has gotta be a violation. Especially the homemade variety. I'd thought it was the prepackaged shit, which is another reason why I didn't look into it.

No one mentioned she was doing that to me, baking shit herself. No doubt on premises as she lives there. And no one mentioned the state of the old place. I had a good idea. The entire block is worth nothing more than the potential of the ground it sits on. But with her there, it means I can't do a fucking thing.

One reason I haven't pushed for a harder attack with law is the off chance of it being tied up in court. She can't afford it, but bleeding hearts abound, and some sucker's no doubt going to want to shine up their shingle by good deeding her case. If it went there.

Of course, I can quietly call in the health department, but first I want a look at the setup. And often with the health department they want a payout. It all depends on who you get. I don't normally have to go to this level, so I'm not up to speed. I come in. I lay down money. People give me what I want.

This is different. I feel it. Because she's soft and stubborn and has fucking beliefs. Honestly, it's disgusting.

I'm getting off track.

I've already made some calls to my people. I want them to keep up the pressure, but not to up the ante.

"You're plotting."

I look up. Ryder's there. I totally forgot we were planning on grabbing a bite as he wanted to talk about the goddamn stupid Sinclair inheritance with me.

"I've got a problem I need to solve."

"Stomp it down like usual."

"I'm figuring the best way. She—"

"Hot?" He's suddenly sprawled in a chair in front of my desk looking all sorts of interested. "Stacked hot? Long legged? Blonde?"

"Short, compact, dark-haired, and a bad case of bleeding heart syndrome."

"Jesus Christ, not your type at all. I vote for a blonde. I'll take a redhead. I'm in the mood for a redhead."

"If it's hot and female, you're always in the mood."

"True. There's a lot of me to go around. I'm extremely generous."

"I'm sure. But this is business. This girl's the one thing keeping me from my Bushwick development."

He doesn't say anything, just eyes me thoughtfully. "No one gets in your way."

"She won't budge. She's got morals and beliefs."

"Sounds horrendous," he says, deadpan.

"Asshole."

"Hey, I'm your favorite brother."

"No, you're not. That would be Hud and King."

He clutches his chest. "You wound me."

"See, they're into making money." I stop. "Make that Kingston. Hud's gone soft."

"Hey, I love making money. Almost as much as I love hitting great pussy."

I laugh and shake my head. The rain's stopped, but clouds still hang low outside in the sky. I get up and grab my light fall coat and sweep an arm toward the door. My staff's already left for the day, so it's just us and the security in the lobby. I glance at the wrap around window. "You think it's going to rain? I no longer have an umbrella."

And for some reason, I find myself smiling.

After all, today's been a good day. A good beginning.

For me.

For Zoey Smith?

Not so much.

Zoey's wearing a dress the next morning. It's a pretty one, and it compliments her eyes, which are a dark blue, almost violet.

She's not my type. Way too fucking sweet and smiling and little. I like tall and curves and less talking. I like a mouth that can do things to my body, and a woman who knows when to get the fuck out. Which is after sex.

I'm not Ryder. I'm not a wham bam kinda guy. I don't need a different woman every time to spice up my life. But women serve a need. A certain kind of woman. Sometimes I'll see them for a while because the sex is that good, but they always get clingy, or start picturing themselves with a Mrs. before their first name, followed by a Sinclair. Even the ones with money.

My favorite women I date and sleep with are the cutthroat variety. The ones who are playing hardball, who have needs like mine and don't want anything else.

But those relationships tend to last a few months at the most because we always have different schedules that prove harder to coordinate than need. And for both me and for them, there's always someone more available around the corner.

No complications is what I'm on about here.

Zoey Smith looks like she was built out of complications.

If she were my type.

Which she isn't.

She's pretty enough, and her mouth is soft and sweet and would look good wrapped about my cock. I don't want her, but I'll admit I'm enough like Ryder to sum up the fuckability of a female without thinking about it.

Actually, I don't know why I'm thinking about it.

Maybe it's the way the dress shows off her small waist, or the neckline hints at her modest cleavage.

Or the rosy glow to her cheeks that no doubt came from her running around earlier. She was probably out feeding the homeless. If there were lepers, no doubt she'd be there, ready to help.

I'm being a bit of a bastard. Maybe she doesn't give a shit about lepers. I haven't asked. I don't intend to.

Right, I need to get my mind on track, back to my nonexistent dear old gran. And the plight of my made up life.

I need to find out more of Zoey's weaknesses, and thinking of sex and her bleeding heart isn't going to help.

She hooks a curl behind an ear and smiles up at me. "I've been up baking a storm since four am," she says by way of explanation to the boxes of books sitting on the floor. "And I forgot I had a small shipment coming in."

"Where do you get the books from?"

"Estate sales sometimes. Other times, people donate. And when I have time—I try to take time once a month—I poke about the tristate area. You'd be surprised what lurks in the strangest of places."

"Like under trees?" I look at her, picking up a couple of hard covers from an open box. I've never heard of these authors. Where are the blockbusters? The known writers? She clearly has no idea what the fuck she's doing.

If she did, she'd have sold to me at the first offer.

"Junk shops, garage sales—"

"Secondhand bookshops, am I right?"

The color in her cheeks heightens. "Sometimes. I actually occasionally get some new books in. I'll set up over here and, and then I can show you around. I open in an hour so we should have time."

I frown. "Your door was unlocked."

"I didn't know when you'd turn up, or if you would." She comes up and puts one hand on the books I'm holding. "I never got any of your details or told you how much."

"That doesn't matter."

Now she frowns, and I realize I've said the wrong thing. Of course it matters. Or it would, if I were actually Magnus Simpson. Shit.

I take a breath. "I mean, I'm just grateful to have a job that gives me time to help Gran."

"I never told you the hours."

"You said part time, and..." I'm going to have to skirt a little closer to the truth, use it to get to her. I'm here to learn her weaknesses, what makes her tick, find the way to get her to sell. I'm not really sure what that is, but I do know I'm good at puzzles and spending time day to day's going to give me that key.

"And honestly?" I look at Zoey again. "I'm just happy to have anything. Whatever hours you have, I can make work. Whatever you pay, I can make work. I have some savings, I just need extra to help Gran. You know..."

"I do. And I'm so sorry you're going through this. If I had a million dollars, I'd give it to you."

"You don't know me."

"I like to help. I don't see the point of hoarding money or things if you can't share and spread the goodness. I sound like an idiot, I know, but it's true. There's enough in the world to make everyone's lives better."

"One woman can't save the planet."

"Maybe, but sometimes, all it takes is one person doing one small thing. So... that's my aim."

I'm really not sure what to say. So I just nod and smile.

"So before we open—"

"You want the resume? IRS details?"

Her eyes get big. "Not the last. I mean..." She drops her voice and says, "You're struggling so I'll pay under the table for now and later we can talk. But take care of your gran first. I can't pay a lot. Fifteen an hour? Is that good? We can do... say ...twenty or twenty-five hours a week?"

She has zero business sense. But I smile and place one hand against my chest. "You're an angel, Zoey. My resume got wet yesterday, but I'll give it to you so you have my number."

I walk past her, deftly pulling the books she has her hand on away from her and to the counter. Setting them down, I retrieve the resume. It's a little mangled. I didn't think much beyond shifting it to today's jeans. Magnus Simpson, I've decided, is just as soft as her, and he's also so caught up in caring for Gran that he really isn't thinking about making a perfect impression.

After all, he'd never be in this poky hole-in-the-wall if he was.

She comes over to me, her head barely reaching my shoulder. And I'm met with a hint of violets and spice that are both understated, sexy, romantic, and old fashioned. It suits her. "Oh, good. Your number's still clear on it. I'll program it in to my phone and here." She stretches across the counter, narrowly missing a glass covered plate with what looks like cake inside. There are cookies, too, further back. But these are dark, almost black, and no doubt full of chocolate and sugar. It's a wonder a man doesn't get diabetes walking into this place.

Zoey hands me a little card. It's very simple. Just the shop name, hers, and a phone number. Just the one. I slide it into my pocket.

"I'll show you around."

We weave in among the narrow high shelves and Zoey points out the little sections for different books. Sale items, fiction, lit, women's fiction, minority voices, art, history—it goes on and up the stairs that have piles of books on them here and there. The place is a death trap.

Maybe I'll call the fire department.

Of course, she'd probably feed them cake and cookies and they'd fall into a sugar coma and wake, forgetting why they'd come here.

Upstairs is another floor of books, but it's a little more open, a big arched window in the front of the floor, and an open space with some comfy chairs and a sofa and a table with books. There are even lamps and a rug.

I want to eye her with disgust. She's made a reading area. This isn't a library, for crying out loud. No wonder she's harried and talking about tough times. Dear fucking God. She's a mess.

"I love this little space," she says, eyes shining. "I was going to have it full of books up here, too. This used to be a storage area and my grandpa had a hardware store downstairs, but when he retired, it got turned into a dollar store to the people it was rented to, and when my grandparents passed, and the people renting closed up, well...I figured it was time for me to open my dream."

"This store?"

She nods, and smiles dreamily. "I don't know where I'd be without books. They're magic."

"Like the sign?"

"Yes. And I thought of having a place where people can peruse in comfort, or just escape and read something, no matter if they buy, then it would all be worth it."

Money. That would be worth it.

"I know it might sound stupid."

It does. "No, not at all," Magnus Simpson, all round good guy and sucker says.

"And who knows? Maybe people mention it to others, and a book gets sold down the line."

Downstairs the bell dings. And she grabs my arm, sending sparks of fire through me. I put it down to static electricity from the rug. "Come on, Magnus, time to get started."

I follow her down the stairs, making sure not to touch her again.

This is going to be like stealing candy from a baby.

# Chapter Four

## ZOEY

How a man can get sexier is beyond me, but he has. And dripping wet Magnus was scorching. Dry Magnus is better. Maybe it's because that dimple shows a little more each time he smiles, or he listens to me.

Listens and doesn't run.

Of course, he'd like money, so he's not about to run, but still...

I wipe suddenly sweaty hands down the sides of my dress. The Sinclair thugs came again last night as I was about to lock the door. The same offer as before, but this time they'd left without their usual Cult-level tenacity.

I've left him to unpack and price and shelve the books. The pricing is easy as I sorted the boxes and marked the tops of the boxes. He should be fine with that.

Downstairs is Mrs. O'Reilly, a buxom African American woman whose husband, Mr. O'Reilly, runs a bar over on the next block.

"Zoey."

She marches up to the counter, a powerhouse in a cap that perpetually sits over her setting hair.

"Dark chocolate with white chocolate chunks and pecans, and a slice of hibiscus lemon drizzle cake."

"I didn't come for that!" She puts her bag immediately in her handbag and nabs the extra cookie I set on a plate for her. "Declan is beside himself."

Declan—or Mr. O'Reilly—is always like that, according to her. He's the most mild mannered and even keeled man I've met, but she loves a touch of drama in her life so I indulge. "Oh no." I select another slice of cake and a cookie and bag those. "To calm his nerves."

"You're a good girl. No, he's worried about what this construction will do to business. It's already down with the closures and people having to move out." Her voice drops to a loud whisper. "Apparently, people don't want to spend money on drinks because they're worried about finding something affordable, you hear me?"

"If I have my way, there won't be people moving. I'm staying."

She pats my hand. "You don't have to tell me. But the rest? They're weak." She practically quivers with outrage.

"If the worst happens, O'Reilly's is going to be just fine. Construction crews love a drink after work."

She sighs and devours her cookie, then eyes the rest behind the counter. "I hope you're right. Now, if the worst happens, come work your baking witchcraft at the bar."

"I said I'll bake for you when I have time," I say.

"You got a lot going on here." She looks about.

I set the espresso machine up for two cups, and then I pack the rarely used single cup section and set that, too. "Anytime you need help, Mrs. O, you ask."

"I just came by to let you know the trains are all screwy today, so don't you go nowhere, you hear? You could get stuck in that devil place."

"Manhattan?"

"Yes."

I bite my lip to stop laughing. I don't know what happened to her in Manhattan, but she despises it. "Oh, your LaWanda Stevens are in."

"New?"

"At secondhand neighbor prices. As well as some of the ones you mentioned a while ago you haven't read."

She's off, powering down the romance section. "Now these are what I'm talking about! Books about real women. With curves. Ooh, he's handsome."

The men on the covers are always handsome. And LaWanda romances are about women like her and she loves them. She told me she hates the ones about blondes built like twigs who'd break in a soft breeze, and I don't think she was talking about the heroines.

She returns with a pile of books and I bag and ring them up. "Ten dollars."

"Do you know," she says, fishing out a bunch of ones, "there's a dreamboat stacking books back down that aisle."

It's her low, conspiratorial voice, so I'm positive Magnus heard every word.

Her gaze is back on the cookies and I give her a cup of espresso with copious cream and five sugars—it's definitely more sugar and cream than caffeine and another cookie. "It might storm, too."

She says this like that's what we've been talking about and Magnus comes over.

There's a look in his dark onyx eyes that makes my stomach perform complicated flip flops as he does so, but then he smiles a little hesitantly and my dumb heart flutters because he looks slightly lost and sheepish.

"I've finished the books."

"Mrs. O'Reilly, this is Magnus. Magnus, Mrs. O'Reilly. I just hired him."

Okay, it's more he hired himself, but semantics...

She doesn't wait for him to offer his hand; she grabs it and shakes it hard. She's a strong woman, but he takes it in his stride. "Pleased to meet you."

"Ooh, Declan better step up his game, girl. That's all I'm saying."

She finishes her coffee and then I give her another cookie and she takes her bag and swans out the door, into the gray morning.

"Mrs. O'Reilly is... interesting," he says, amusement running warm through his voice.

"She is. And she's sweet."

His eyebrow raises, but he doesn't say anything.

I hand him an espresso and take mine and add milk and sugar and then pop a cookie on a plate for him. He didn't have one yesterday, but I'm sure that's just because it was a job interview. Only monsters and people named Sinclair hate cookies.

Fine, I don't know if the last one is true, but I imagine it is. He takes the coffee and has a sip. Outside, the sky growls.

"Usually today is slow, so I stock and then dust and do all kinds of things. I'll show you the register." I stop and lift my gaze to him which is a little too easy to do. I know I need to stop secretly ogling him because I'm his boss. But it's hard, he's just so hot. "Unless you know how to use one. You probably do—"

"I don't."

"Oh." I frown and play with my cup. "Didn't you do an afterschool job?"

"Not one behind a register. It's okay, I'm a fast learner."

"Come around here."

He does and I can barely breathe. How did I not notice there's almost no space here? The heat of him seeps into me and he smells as divine as he did yesterday, that citrusy whiskey scent that teases and flirts. He's probably married. I slide my gaze down to his hands. No ring. They're beautiful hands, strong, capable, elegant.

I tell myself to breathe and start pointing out how to use the register. We go over it about five times and then I open the screen, select test, and then gesture for him to have a go.

"You know, I saw the modern register, but I pegged this place as having an old fashioned kind."

I laugh, our hands brushing as I guide him through this part of the register and a shower of sweet heat washes through me from the brief and fleeting contact.

"Those things are temperamental and expensive. And this is old, second-hand, and cheap."

"Like everything here."

The words shouldn't hurt because I don't think he meant them the way they sounded. But that cheap part... it hurts. My good friend Suzanne said the same thing when I set this place up based on nothing but meager savings and a hell of a lot of sweat and tears and the blood and bones of a decaying relationship.

"Well. Just have a go with it. We're quiet now, so I'll just let you practice." I look around as I edge out from behind the counter, suddenly crowded. My shop isn't much, I guess.

It could use a paint job and the signs that I painted by hand because I couldn't afford to pay for a professional suddenly no longer look charming. They look, well, cheap. And I could clean the window. I used to have a guy, but he moved out of the area a few months ago and I never got around to finding someone else. I know Mikey could use some cash. I guess I can try and stretch things a little further, see if he wants to do the windows weekly.

There's another crack of thunder and it's followed by a sheet of lightning that flashes bright.

Magnus comes up behind me. His wavery reflection in the window gives him away even though he walks silently. He puts his hand on my shoulder. It's warm and comforting and I turn. "I'm sorry. I should have been watching and helping. Is something wrong?"

"Yeah." He flashes the dimple briefly and I ignore the weakness in my knees. But his gaze seems to look down deep into me, like he can see my secrets. I don't have any, but if I did, he'd see them.

"Don't worry, any mistakes won't mess up the books. You're in practice mode."

He frowns. "Not the register, Zoey. You."

"Me?"

"Yeah, I said cheap and I didn't mean—"

"You did and it is. Truth is, I don't have the money to make it splashy." I wander over to the first aisle and start straightening the books, tracing the spines with a finger. "But I don't want this flashy. This isn't a big chain bookstore. It's mine, and it's little and bells and whistles won't do anything. People come in for books."

"And all the sugar you give away."

"Sugar is an important food group."

He goes to say something, but shakes his head. "You're a pushover, Zoey. That woman could afford to buy all the cookies she scarfed, and you charged her ten bucks for fifteen books."

"She's a neighbor."

"With the same name as the bar on the other corner."

I press my lips together. "I run my business my way, Magnus. I know you worked in marketing and it's probably all about flash and the sale and money, but I'm not. I like helping out. She likes my books and the sweets."

"And there was Mikey yesterday."

"He's a kid. I give him books to feed his mind and pad out his lunch box for school by feeding his soul. I'd rather he eat some homemade baked goods than a Twinkie."

"He probably eats both. He's what? Fourteen? Fifteen? Do you know the kind of appetites boys that age have?"

"I'm an only child."

"You're lucky," he mutters.

"You have siblings?"

Before he can answer, the doorbell dings and thunder rolls and I greet my new customer with a smile. "Come on, Magnus. If this guy buys something he can be your first sale."

I make chit chat with the man and answer all his questions. I keep waiting for Magnus to chime in, but he doesn't. He just watches. I'm a little surprised, but then again he doesn't know where everything is, so I just lead the man off in search of his World War books.

Magnus mangles the sale so badly that I end up giving the guy a deep discount. And a cookie. And a slice of cake.

The day wears on and he doesn't really improve and I keep running around like I have three jobs instead of the one.

The only thing Magnus gets is the espresso machine. It's like he's never stepped foot in a lowly store before in his life, and I put it all down to first day jitters. Not to mention worry about his gran.

I'm about to let him go early when the sky cracks loud with thunder and the place lights up supernova bright. And the heavens open.

People scatter on the street and soon it's only the few brave souls dashing about on whatever important business they have because umbrellas don't seem to be much good against this type of downpour.

"Do you want to go?" The sky grows even darker and it's not even four p.m. I thread my hands together, feeling bad because he didn't arrive with an umbrella. "It's pretty bad out there, but..."

"I can stay." He doesn't sound bothered.

"You can call your gran. Let her know you're on your way, or if you want to wait until it lets up, that you'll be late."

"Who?" He stops, stares at me. "Sorry," he says with a laugh, "I thought you said Brad."

"Who's Brad?"

"I don't know."

I stare back and then start laughing. "Good to know that's not her name."

"She's not expecting me today."

"Oh. I thought she was living with you."

"Just nearby." He turns, picks up the feather duster and studies the feathers like he's never seen one before. "I told her I'd be in tomorrow, as I didn't know when I'd finish today."

"Well, I'll make her a special bag of treats, in case you decide to drop by tonight," I say as I slip back behind the counter, feeling a little safer with something between us. Not that he's about to try anything. It's me. He's just so lovely to look at that I'm afraid I might do something embarrassing, like swoon or accidentally on purpose brush against that fine, tight ass. And I don't ever do anything like that. I've turned into a freak. I'm going to have to fire him. I almost start to laugh again but force myself to stop because cackling over nothing is definitely a freak move and I do actually need the help.

I open the register and peer in at the pile of little receipts. Oh lord, there's one for two thousand dollars. I know we didn't sell a truck of books. I'm going to need to hire someone to help me with my new employee.

Magnus is flipping the duster in his hand and he comes up and leans against the counter, leaving a shower of dust as he thumps down the duster. Thank God the treats are under cover or else I'll have to sell them with a special, er, dusting.

We chat back and forth about nothing as the rain slams down and I'm reaching for a cookie because I forgot lunch when the bell dings. My heart plummets as a giant umbrella pokes in shaking water on the floor, followed closely by a man in a dark pinstripe suit and wet shoes.

"Oh no."

Magnus has a strange expression on his face as he straightens up. "Trouble?"

"It's a development heavy, trying to make me sell up."

The man comes up to us.

And then the thug in a suit looks at Magnus and says, "Hey, boss."

# Chapter Five

## MAGNUS

Well fuck. I make a memo to fire Georgio the moment I get back to the office, but instead, I settle on non-verbal communication in the form of a fierce glare.

Georgio starts, then smooths a hand down his tie, and looks at little Zoey. "Boss Lady."

I almost groan. I'm surrounded by idiots.

"The rain drag you out of the hole in the ground you slither about in?" she asks, cold and fierce and dripping with sarcasm.

For a little thing that's got the biggest bleeding heart I've had the misfortune to meet, she's got balls. And claws. I'm impressed against my will.

I almost want to let him put the hard lean on her, or the buttery goodness of a sweet offer, but would Magnus Simpson do that? I've decided Magnus with his old gran is made along similar lines to her, except he's grounded in reality, from this planet. Zoey? I got no fucking idea where she hails from, but it isn't planet Earth.

But right now, I think since I've done pretty much the bare minimum of competent work, I need to ingratiate myself to her. I figure I might work on undermining the business from the inside—that is, when sweet little Zoey isn't doing that to herself—while also presenting as something like a knight in shining armor.

I know Georgio well enough to know he'll follow my lead, and I did ask him to stop by today, but I thought I'd be long gone and I didn't expect him to come out in the torrential downpour that makes yesterday's rain look like a tiny sun shower.

I step up and place myself half between them. "I can handle this for you," I say.

But Zoey puts her hand on my arm and damn if I don't feel her touch all the way down to my dick, and she shakes her head, her wild black curls bouncing and catching the light. "I can do it. But thank you."

"You sure? It'll be my pleasure to escort the thug out."

Georgio looks a little hurt at this. "Just doing my job." His gaze skitters past me to her. "You're gonna be selling up, anyway, so I'm suggesting you take this deal."

"I don't respond well to threats."

"Hear that?" I say, "she doesn't respond well to threats."

"It wasn't a threat."

"It was," she says, all kinds of indignant.

"The lady begs to differ."

"The lady's got a screw loose," Georgio mutters under his breath and I can't argue with that.

Zoey's hand tightens and she comes up close, her breasts brushing against me and they're soft and warm and fuck, now I'm imagining them all naked. Like, are her nipples small, or big? The areole a sweet, soft brown, or pink? Or maybe a dark rose and silver dollar size and... that is not helping my dick out at all. I don't even know why I'm thinking about her tits. I need to get laid is what I need, and her lovely palm-sized breasts aren't on my menu. I like them—not hers.

"I do not. I just don't want to sell and there's no law that says I have to."

There isn't, but given time I'm sure I can pay someone to make one up. But underhanded is one thing, downright illegality is another and doing that definitely plays with illegal and I pride myself on keeping things on the right side of the law. I don't give a fuck about the nitty gritty of morality, but law, yeah.

Besides, I'm not sure she's going to sell unless I can find a way to do that as Magnus Simpson.

"It's not about the law, it's about being smart. My boss is a hard man—"

"He's the devil's younger brother and twice as ugly," she says, "and I really don't care. He can try whatever. I'm not selling."

"Do you know how much this place is worth?"

I stare at Georgio. He did not just say that. Next time, I may as well give him a gun so he can damn well shoot himself in the foot for real.

His eyes bug at the expression on my face and it's a good thing sweet smelling, soft Zoey can't see me. "I—I mean," he says, "The project. You'll be paid well."

"You can offer me the Taj Mahal, but I'll turn you down."

"What she said," I say. "Maybe you should go, talk to your boss. See what he has to say."

"I'll be back."

And Georgio stumbles back, grabs the umbrella, and rushes out into the downpour. A huge crack of thunder accompanies his exit.

Zoey squeals out a delighted little sound and rushes round to stand in front of me, her eyes shining. Like that, smiling, she's exceptionally lovely. And then she throws her arms about me, hugging me tight. "Thank you."

I'm so shocked by this armful of warm female I wrap my arms about her. Fuck, she feels good. She has long legs and it's like she fits. The heat of her melts down into me and there's a flicker of arousal inside, a lick of flame.

"Oh my God." She pulls free, breathing hard, her face red. "I'm sorry... I didn't. I shouldn't. I hugged you."

Zoey says this like she tried to hump my leg.

"I noticed."

She buries her face in her hands. "I'm the worst boss. I wasn't harassing you sexually."

"You can."

She lifts her head and for a long beat neither of us says a word. But Zoey's shock and confusion melts into humor and a smile and she laughs. "That's a joke. Not that I thought it wasn't. I shouldn't have hugged you."

I touch her shoulder, a little shocked I want to draw her back and hold her again, or trace the lines of her mouth to see if it's as soft and inviting as it looks.

I definitely need to get laid.

"It's fine," I say. "And I don't feel harassed, sexually or otherwise. I'm a grown ass man and I can tell the difference between a come on and a hug."

She breathes out a sigh. "I could have handled that, but you were pretty spectacular."

"I'm sure you have men falling all over themselves to white knight for you."

Zoey looks about. "Maybe they're hiding or shy. No, no one, just me. But that was nice of you. That one only comes in when he's wielding big guns and offers. There are actual thugs who threaten to make things hard for me. And others, too. Normally, it takes forever to get rid of them." She pauses. "Weird how he called you boss."

Yeah, real weird. We're gonna have words, big, hard, harsh words, me and Georgio. "He called you the same."

"Chauvinism. That's what it is."

"Calling you boss?"

"He never has before." She crosses her arms and taps her foot as the storm rages outside. "It's because you're here. He thought you were somehow in charge, even though he knows my name's on it. Ooh, I wish that coward Sinclair would show his ugly, fat face. I'd give him a piece of my mind."

"You'd probably feed him cake."

"I would not!" Zoey slowly smiles and starts to straighten up on the aisles facing us. I lean back against the counter as she does so. She has hummingbird energy. It fits her, delicate and robust, still and energetic. A certain kind of beauty to those movements as she hovers busily.

"Well," she says sheepishly, "I might. I offered that oaf a cookie the first time he came. Ate it, too. Kept eyeing them each time. Except today. Probably shocked there was a man there. But! I'd only offer Sinclair stale cake."

"Not poisoned?"

"I'm not evil," she says, throwing a slightly evil look at me.

"Why not sell, Zoey? I've only been here a day, but you work hard and you said you own the building?"

Spots of color darken her cheeks. I know I've stepped a little too far. I need to reel it back in, take it slowly. Clearly, I'd prefer this settled now so I can concentrate on all the other steps, but we're months from even thinking of bringing a building down. Still, I like to have everything set in advance. I have plans and time schedules set up and the way forward, the only way, is brutal efficiency and making sure things go like clockwork.

So, I may have to make underhanded moves like this to push it along.

Sure, it's called underhanded for a reason, but I'm not breaking laws, and she'll get over it.

Zoey will be crushed, but there's always fallout. And it's not like it will kill her. I'm setting her free from the shackles of thankless work for nothing, of no doubt scraping the bottom of the barrel to keep the fucking lights on.

Shit, I'd bet myself a million bucks she can't afford to pay me, but I'm betting she also needs someone to help here. The taxes alone will be astronomical for her since she doesn't have tenants. And this is classed as a business, so the majority of utilities will cost more, and I'm actually beginning to bore myself.

I shift my mind back to her, and how her ass looks as she bends to fix the books on the bottom shelf. It's one sweet ass. Not big, but perfect to cup when kissing or fucking her against a wall.

And there I go again. Thinking of sex and Zoey and things that shouldn't even go together in my mind.

But there's something about her that creeps under the skin when a man isn't looking and it's probably called not being laid in over two weeks. I had to cancel a date because I was so damn busy with all this and I parted ways with the last regular lady with benefits I had on account she got the vice president job she wanted and moved to LA.

Great for Jane, seriously, but sometimes it's good to have ease of access on tap.

Picking up isn't an issue, but it takes time to find someone that I want, and Jesus, I'm sounding like my brother, Ry.

"I don't want to sell," she says, straightening up. "That's giving in."

"Is it? I'm not talking myself out of a job, just playing a little devil's advocate, but you could buy three stores with what they're offering."

She frowns and comes toward me. "How do you know what they're offering? I never said and Sinclair's goon didn't have any paperwork out."

Fuck. Mr. Nice Guy here has a problem with his mouth, apparently. I don't usually just talk like this with loads of free time. Because this isn't a job, it's fucking about. My days are jam-packed from six a.m. until nine p.m. most days. This... this is unlike anything I've ever done. I'm about making, not wasting, money. I don't shoot shit and I don't spend time in musty bookstores with pretty little pint-sized females whose hearts are way too big for their health.

I shrug and keep it deliberately casual. "He said it was a good deal or something, so I just assumed."

She lifts a hand to her forehead and gives a small smile. "I'm just over it. I'm not selling. This place has been in the family for decades and... my heart and soul are soaked into these walls. People have always told me what I can't do, or what's better and easier for me, but you know what? I've never been happier than having this store. I think I already told you all this, or maybe I didn't."

"You can tell me anything."

The real Magnus prefers slinking out of rooms when people get like this. I don't enjoy it and I don't have the time. I almost decide my fictional gran needs me, but it's still snarling, fighting cats and dogs outside and besides, the fake Magnus would listen. Because the fake Magnus is going to get all the ammunition I need to bring her down.

"It's hard, I won't lie, keeping this place going, but it means so much and I'm so proud of it. I love it's a nice little slice of history and that people can come here. I like that this is one of the last bastions of a dying old school Brooklyn. It's not much to look at, but it's mine."

There's no dramatic countenance in her words, or even some higher purpose. They're just full of quiet dignity and love and steel.

"So nothing would ever make you sell."

"I'd give a kidney if someone asked. And if someone absolutely, desperately needed money and selling this was the only way to save them, then I would. In a heartbeat."

It's wrong. I know it is. But as she says those words, it hits me.

Somehow, someway, little Zoey is going to sell.

To save me.

Or... fictional gran.

It would almost be delicious if it wasn't such a diabolical plan.

# Chapter Six

## ZOEY

By the end of the day, no customers have come in since the heavens opened and the goon left. I peer anxiously at the deepening gray and the non-stop rain. He's there behind me. I can see him, a wavery large figure behind me in the glass that runs with rivulets.

"Hot date?"

I almost laugh at that. I can't really remember when I last had a date, hot or otherwise.

"No. Just thinking…"

He sighs, his fingers dancing lightly, fleetingly, over my shoulder, sending little shivers of awareness racing hot through my blood.

"Probably of firing me."

I turn, but he doesn't step back and we're close. His heat surrounds me, along with his evocative scent that twines with the ever present smell of old books, and twists into something that makes my mouth water. I tip my face to him. "No. You're sparkly new. The wrapper's only just come off. You'll get the hang of it."

He smiles and threads a curl behind my ear, his fingers lingering a moment. "I hope so. You don't know what this means to me."

Magnus looks like he wants to say more, but doesn't, and instead he moves back and I follow him, down through the aisles of books as he straightens them even though they'll never be straight. And it's not like we've had teeming throngs of people in here, pawing over everything. Not with the rain and the storm. Not like that ever happens, anyway.

"Your gran?"

He doesn't look at me, almost like he's embarrassed. "Something like that. Yeah."

I take a breath and lean against the Westerns. "Life has a way of working out."

"Are you always some kind of eternal optimist?" He cuts me a quick glance, long fingers moving over the spines of old thrillers.

"Not really," I say. It's a bit of a lie, but if I admit that, I'll sound like some kind of sickening Pollyanna type. "I just don't see the point of letting things you can't change get you down. Proactive is the way ahead."

"Yeah, I can see that." He pulls out a book and pushes it back into its place. "Anyway, I should go."

"You're welcome to stay until this madness outside stops."

"I'm a big boy, I can take it." And he straightens, moves slowly past me, almost brushing me, and the slide of air between our bodies is like a gossamer kiss and I can barely breathe.

At the end of the aisle, he stops and the look he gives me makes my heart lurch. There's something else going on, I can see that, like words dance on his tongue, but he won't give them voice. But it isn't my business. We don't know each other. Not yet. I don't want to chase him off.

He's about to turn the corner into the center of the store and I find myself following. "Magnus, we don't... I mean, you and I don't know each other that well, but if you need anything, you know, even someone to sit with your gran or bring soup or something, let me know."

He smiles, and it's sad, and he just says, "You gave me a job."

It's not until long after he's gone I realize he forgot the treats.

Magnus Simpson is smart, gorgeous, complex and has no idea what he's doing.

It's a few days later, evening, and I'm ready for bed. The skies are still heavy but no rain and Magnus…well…

He can't use the register without making me work about three hours untangling the mess at the end of the day, and he also isn't great at sales. Not that I'm into pushing people into buying things, which is good because otherwise I'd have to fire him.

But he's great at organizing my shelves and he listens to me and I've also noticed an uptick in people coming in over the past few days.

By people, I mean females. Even the ones old enough to be his gran.

And they all make eyes at him.

I understand that, because it's an easy thing to do.

Maybe he's not great at his job because his mind is elsewhere, like on his gran. I keep going back to the conversation during the storm, the night he stood so close and made my stomach perform slow, sweeping loop the loops, when he touched my hair and looked at me with a softness, and the way he wouldn't look at me, like he held something in.

Not about me. I'm not that girl, even though every so often I catch him looking at me, like there's another layer, like there's something… maybe something he wants to say, but doesn't.

I make a hot chocolate, a secret vice and add extra marshmallows, even though it isn't the hot chocolate season. I sip it as I fuss around the cozy but no-fuss apartment above the store.

Another reason I don't want to sell.

Memories live and breathe in here. My family, my grandparents, and everyone who breathed life into this place and helped form it to what it is today.

Home.

A piece of old New York.

After the hot chocolate's gone and everything is locked and done for the evening, I set out the recipes I'll make first thing. I found an old bakery book in the last haul. I'm reading that tonight, and I'll find something in there. It's from the turn of last century and those recipes are always fun to play with and tweak.

I pull back the covers and slide into bed, holding the book. Tomorrow is the block meeting at O'Reilly's, so I have a lot going on. With a yawn, I flick through the book, but my eyes are heavy and I'm reaching for the light when my phone buzzes.

"Suzanne," I say after checking my caller ID. "What's up?"

"I have a party to go to tomorrow, if you want to come along. You know, if you're not all up in your silly store's business."

A tick of annoyance pings in me. Honestly, sometimes I wonder if we hadn't met at college if we'd be friends. She comes from money, has a sweet duplex in the West Village, and a sweeter job at her father's company doing... something.

But she's got a good heart under all the snobbery. I sigh. "I found someone to work part time, so I'm training him."

"Him? Do tell." She practically purrs the words. "Unless he's been hit with the ugly, then don't."

I roll my eyes up to the shadowed ceiling as traffic squeals outside and shouts of an altercation ring out in the air. "He's cute, if you like that sort of thing. But you know, he works for me."

"So? It's time we took back the work space."

"I don't think so."

"The party, you should come."

I hate those kind of things. Besides, my job and saving my building takes up most of my time.

But Suzanne is sometimes easiest to handle by noncommittal vagaries. "Where is it?"

"Grab a pen!"

I jot it down faithfully, along with her instructions on what to wear. Then the sighs. "I am busy tomorrow, Suze, but I'll try."

"Saving the condemned? That's not a thing, that's torture, now, listen to this. I met this guy..."

And closing my eyes, I settle back for the story.

All the prices are wrong.

I don't know how that happened, because I marked all the boxes and my instructions were clear. But when Magnus comes in, it's like he's got a sixth sense because even though I swear I'm my usual easy, breezy self, he suddenly straightens, like he's the one in charge, zeroing in on a problem he needs to handle.

"What happened, Zoey?"

His poor, frail gran comes to my head. I turn up the smile wattage. "Nothing. Cookie?"

He catches my arm as I go to slide by him, and though his hold isn't tight, it's firm and his touch sends tendrils of heat through me, coiling and spinning in my blood. Those onyx eyes are intense on me and it's suddenly difficult to breathe.

Because that mouth of his is rich with life, and made for kissing.

I jerk back at the thought, but he doesn't let go.

"I made macadamia, cacao, and pumpkin seed spiced cookies. High protein, full of healthy things."

"Sugar?" Suddenly his gaze softens. "No. I just want to know what's up."

"There's the meeting tonight about the bully of a billionaire's take over, that's all, and—"

"I don't think it's that." He softens a little more. "If it's me, tell me what to do to improve to keep the job."

"It's not in danger."

"If I'm not doing a good job, it should be."

"You're fine." It's really hard to breathe and his thumb is drawing slow circles on my inner arm and the sparks those touches set off are like low lying electricity. "It's just..."

Everything.

"Some of the books have been priced incorrectly."

"You don't charge enough."

I go still. "Did you misprice them on purpose?"

For a long moment he doesn't answer, then he drops his hand to his side and shrugs, looking sheepish and the whole intense moment is gone. "God, sorry, Zoey. I didn't mean... I just thought the prices were old ones. I thought I was helping."

"Well... ask."

At that moment, the bell dings and someone comes in and the day begins.

Magnus is still there when I rush downstairs to make the meeting. We had a glut, and by that, I mean seven people right at the end of the day, each fussier and more indecisive than the last.

Normally, I don't mind, but I want to get to the meeting.

I stop and stare. He's got a feather duster in his hand and there's some jazz playing low.

Magnus turns and gives a soft whistle. "All dressed up."

"I put on lipstick. And heels. Low heels."

"So I see." The dimple appears.

"I thought you'd gone."

"Well, I felt bad about the books, so I decided to do some cosmetic work."

I raise a brow. "Dusting?"

"Dusting." He looks about, then scratches his chin with the duster handle. "Zoey, do you want some company tonight?"

"Like a date?" The moment the words hit the air I want the ground to eat me. "No, of course not a date. Why would you want to go on a date with me? I'm your boss, and..." I stop. "Let's pretend I didn't just say all that."

He smiles slow and my knees turn weak. "If you like."

"But what about your gran?"

"See, the thing there is, you have to play it low key." A dark shadow crosses his face. "She's independent, and... I don't want her to think I'm hovering."

"But she needs you."

"Gran is proud and stubborn, and I drop in. I help her out. But the money... with the money I can... I can help." He sighs. "At least a little."

Questions push at me, but I don't ask. Even though I desperately want to. "You should go have some fun."

He nods, but doesn't look at me.

The man's a walking Adonis. Women drool over him. Myself included. He can't be lonely.

Then again, maybe with his gran and his opting to focus on her, maybe he is. Maybe he just wants a distraction.

Because I'm suspecting it's not just his gran is old and injured, but there's something else there he's not talking about.

"Magnus, I'd love some company."

He grins and I almost demand smelling salts and swoon it's so disarming and gorgeous. "I'll get my coat."

"That was...interesting. Haven't most of them sold?"

People are out and about, going places. This isn't a party central, happening place in Brooklyn. Too many hoods that loiter, too many empty and nailed up places.

I shrug and step over a broken bottle. "Most are in negotiations."

"You're the outlier. Wouldn't it be easier for them if you sold?"

I give him a sharp look. "People who own can sell, and most have who want to just take the money and run. Others want to stay but don't have a choice. You heard them."

"Cities live and breathe and change. This place needs an injection."

I stop and glare at him. "This place is having the oxygen sucked out. Let's get this straight. The Sinclair family—whom I hate, especially this Edward who's behind this. I've heard his name. The coward likes to hide behind his company name, but he's just a pathetic man—is so rich, they don't care about me, they don't care about the neighborhood, they don't care about you. They care about money."

"You met him?"

"No. But people like him are all the same. Crush and destroy everything to make more money they don't need. People here can't afford to go elsewhere, but they'll have to. Further out, probably into worse neighborhoods and those with jobs in Manhattan or around here will have to travel further. Kids will need to change schools. And people will have to either find something else or rebuild. Those who rent their buildings for businesses are also being priced out."

He nods. "This is how the world works, Zoey. You change or you get swallowed."

"I won't change. I won't get swallowed. I'll sit there and they can damn well build around me. They won't. I'll be an eyesore. So—"

"Sometimes it's easier."

"So you'd let your gran just sit alone and you work a fancy job because it's easier?"

A muscle ticks in his jaw, but he nods. "I see your point."

"I'm just…" Hopeless, that's what I am, that feeling slides through me again. I've been told that before. My last boyfriend hated I stayed here, hated the store. "I'm tired. It gets to me. All the sadness and anger. No one thinks they can stand up to big business."

"But you will?"

I smile. "I'm more stubborn than you think."

My phone buzzes. Suzanne.

And suddenly, a really stupid idea comes to me.

"Do you want to go to a party?"

# Chapter Seven

## MAGNUS

The last thing I expected was an invite out. But I take it.

We take the train to Manhattan and honestly, I can't remember the last time I was on public transport. But it's good, because I can now say how easy it is to get from my new enterprise to the city.

So far, my plan's going perfectly.

Little Zoey Smith's aching to ask me about poor gran. I've dropped small hints that there's more going on than an old lady who's had some kind of fall.

The one thing I didn't expect was her reinforced backbone made of titanium. That's Zoey's, not my imaginary gran.

"So where are we going in the East Village?"

This is a place I'm dragged to by Ryder, otherwise I have no interest in this part of Manhattan.

"Avenue A and St. Mark's. My friend Suzanne loves swank and hip parties and I don't."

I stop and look at her. "Not enough cookies?"

Her eyes narrow. "You have something against cookies?"

"They're pointless snacks."

She gasps. "Only a monster would say that."

"Or a man who cares about his health. I drink, so I guess I'm only part monster."

In my head I'm flipping through swank places around here where people might know me, along with anyone by the name Suzanne, but I come up blank.

Besides, any small risk is worth it to spend time with Zoey outside her natural habitat. It allows me to morph the relationship, to mold it into the direction I want it to go, to make her easy to pluck and strip down. Metaphorically. To get her building.

The streets are filled with people and we weave through them until we reach an apartment building perched above the buzzing stores on the corner of Avenue A and St. Marks. It's not much outside, but someone's renovated—cheaply inside. We take the elevator up to the penthouse and it opens on a by the book place that's meant to be classy, but is just overpriced.

A blonde with big tits in a shimmery black dress that's like a second skin swoops down. She falters when she sees me and then flutters her eyelashes. "And who are you?"

Her gaze barely touches on Zoey, which for some reason pisses me the hell off. I don't know why. It's not like I care.

"This is Suzanne," Zoey says.

"I'm Suzanne and you're gorgeous."

I wince. "I'm here with Zoey."

The woman blinks hard, and her head jerks back a little. Just when I'm about to pin a label on her, she flicks it away with a big grin as she looks at her friend. "Good for you, Zo."

Zoey groans. "Don't—"

"Do." I say, instantly interested. I tell myself I'm mining for soft spots and vulnerabilities in the sweet smelling thorn in my side, and I shift closer to Zoey. She's warm and I already know she's soft skinned and with the kind of subtle curves that make a man reconsider his tastes.

Not that I need to. I'm not my brother, but my type is more personality than build.

"Tell me everything."

"Zoey needs to meet a good man."

"Oh does she?"

"She does not," says the subject huffily. "A woman, Suze, contrary to your outmoded opinion, doesn't need a man."

"It's not about need. It's about want."

"Come on, Magnus, let's get a drink. And you..." She pins her friend with a hard stare, "aren't making me come out again."

"Spoilsport. Bye, Magnus..." And she makes a beeline for a hot guy.

The drinks that are lined up in the vast open living room, all decked out in white with touches of silver, are top shelf. At least, the kind of top shelf this lot cares about. It's not my kind of party and judging from the misery edging into the corners of Zoey, it's not her place either.

These people are moneyed. They most likely have high-powered, flashy jobs and they like to show it.

But I'm not interested in them. I'm interested in Zoey. The more I know the more I'm armed against her with my next move. I'm thinking multiple attacks, but my diabolical plan is still front and center in my head.

There's a set of stairs through the kitchen area, and as it's the penthouse and a quick glance outside shows another structure above the deck—New York law means a penthouse must have a certain amount of space given over to roof top access—I'm guessing there's another level.

I grab the bottle of wine Zoey went for earlier that no one else has touched and gesture with my chin to the stairs. "Wanna get some air?"

"Yeah."

The stairs are dusty and gloomy as we climb, and the door heavy that I push open at the top. But as we step out onto the empty, bare bones space, it's worth it, because Zoey unfurls.

She lifts her face to the Manhattan sultry night air and breathes in, letting it out with a sigh and a smile. "Thanks."

"For dragging you off?"

She shakes her head and moves to the railing. We're about the equivalent of nine floors up now, but all around us the city glows and sparkles, the noise of life wafting up and making us both part and apart from it all.

"I'm more comfortable in a bookstore or a dive than here. This isn't my world."

"Then why come?"

She leans forward on the rail, then lifts her glass and takes a deep swallow. "Honestly?"

"Yeah."

"It's the best way to keep Suzanne quiet for a while. We met in college and she's a good friend, don't let her flirting fool you, but we're very different."

"Wait, you studied and she partied?" I top up her drink and add a little to mine.

"No. She partied and studied. But she comes from money and she loves this world. She thinks that I've been single too long and I spend too much time with books over people and I sink my money into a failing project."

Oh, Suzanne, you just might be my new best friend. I make a noncommittal noise.

"I know my store sucks up money, but not everything is about being rich. It's home, and it brings pleasure. It's its own thing, and people like Edward Sinclair could never understand that. Not everything is cookie cutter—"

"Says the woman who owns a lot of cookie cutters."

"I do not. I hand roll them. Unless it's Christmas, and it's not the same thing." Zoey wrapped her hands around her glass as a siren's scream rose up from the streets below. "People like that ugly, fat bully—whom I hate, by the way—"

"Really? I had no idea."

Her eyes narrow. "Are you mocking me?"

"Not at all." I top up our glasses and take a sip. The wine's okay for warming wine, I suppose, but I'm more interested in what Zoey has to say to me in our tiny corner of the world up here.

"It's just people like him don't get it. They have no heart. They want uniform things. It's like all those big box stores. There's a reason New York keeps a lot of them out. They kill the small little neighborhood businesses. They steal."

"I'd argue they don't steal."

"I'm not talking about money, Magnus. I mean the quirkiness of little places. Unique pieces of the world that make it up."

She's wrong, but she's smart, I'll give her that. But her stubbornness can't just be from her bias against big business. Big business gets her books to her on time. It keeps things running. Creates jobs. And I have a heart. It's just not bleeding and soft like hers. Which reminds me, I need to check on my charities and non-profits. Maybe I'll add a school reading program to my list, to help underprivileged kids. I can name it after her.

"People like convenience."

She nods and looks out over the east side and Tompkins Square Park that's across from us. "You sound like my ex."

"Uh oh."

"Bronn's not part of my world and I should have known it."

I stare at her. "Bronn? As in Bronn Lichtenfeld?"

The words are out before I can stop them and her face swings up and she frowns. "How..."

"I think my marketing firm once did a campaign for his." The Lichtenfelds are in big business. Banking. But they also snap up properties. All kinds. They don't care about what they're doing. They're the quintessential amassers of fortune by sheer number and they've always wanted a piece of my family's pie. Get a slice of Sinclair reputation and it's easier to make some questionable investments and purchases in less than stellar environmental circles look better.

That's the thought, anyway. I've never liked Bonn and how he handles his father's company. Comparisons have been made with his philandering ways and Ryder. But that's all they are.

Ryder likes women. A lot of women. He plays fast and loose and no one's gonna pin him down, but when it comes to business, he's scrupulous—his way.

But it puts little Zoey in a different light. The fact he went for her. I didn't think he had it in him to see quality over flash.

"Yeah, well, he's cut from the same cloth as this Sinclair monster," she says darkly. "Probably cheats on her, too."

And there we have it. But while I might go in for the kill, soft Magnus with the ailing, and probably by now on life support, gran wouldn't. He'd be kind and supportive and digging all the information he can in a different way.

"Asshole."

"Exactly." Her shoulders deflate. "It's a long time ago, college, but we were on and off for a few years after. That was me, not him, because I didn't want his life, and he wanted the jets, the high rolling fancy restaurants. I just wanted someone who could be with me. Maybe love me. That was not him."

I sigh and nod and wonder if Magnus should have a wound of the heart, too. "And it still hurts."

"No. He's a jerk. Suzanne thinks I'm still hung up, but I'm not. I dumped him. He cheated and lied and I don't play with that. He didn't get my little store, and he thought a gift to me would be to raze it to the ground, put up a chain bookshop so I could play at running it, and that was my final straw."

I look at her. Stare.

Zoey Smith.

Little, unassuming Zoey Smith.

She's something else.

"You dumped him over the store and not the other women?"

"Well, that didn't help." She gives me a small, rueful smile that, in the shadowy light on this roof top spot, lets her pretty face bloom into something more than I first saw. Like this, with that smile, that self-knowledge and utter artless way she has, makes her beautiful.

"Anyway, Suzanne has a mission to test any man I bring along to make sure he's not the same kind of cheating asshole, and then she bugs me because I don't have time for men. I dated a bit, but it's just hard with the store."

"Is it that important?"

"Yes."

Fire burns in her eyes and something in me stirs.

"I get it." I do, but what I get is far more important than a stupid crumbling store. My important is world's away from hers. Mine is about changing the world, not selling moldy books.

"What about you?"

"I don't have anyone."

"Just your gran?"

I let out a long sigh. "Yeah." Then I shift closer to Zoey. I like being close to her. Her scent is soft, sweet magic. "Have you ever wished you had something so you could just use it to save one small thing?"

"All the time."

"Like your store, huh?"

"I'd give it up in a heartbeat if it was for the right cause." She stops, takes a sip of wine and overhead a plane roars about the yells and shouts and traffic below. "Well, I live there, but I'd risk it, for the right reasons. I'd risk it all. I think anyone would."

"No," I say, taking her glass and setting it down with mine and the bottle. Then I step in, brushing the hair from her face. "I really don't think so."

And then, because I want to, because it just feels right, I lower my mouth to hers.

# Chapter Eight

## ZOEY

Oh my God. Magnus lowers his mouth to mine, his lips, those gorgeous lips that must fuel a thousand female fantasies brush lightly on mine.

It's a sweet, soft, fleeting kiss, a butterfly touch that makes my blood sing arias. His mouth is warm, everything I imagined and more.

I sway in against him, seeking, wanting...

I don't care this is someone I just hired. I don't care I just met him. It's like magic, a light that whispers in my blood, and then, like a dream, it shatters into reality.

"Magnus?" The shout is shocked and the voice low and male.

"Shit." He's not kissing me anymore. Instead, his head jerks up and he glances over my head as the sounds of the city and the light from the door where we stepped through infiltrate my spinning, buzzing head.

I go to turn, but Magnus pulls me to him and looks at me and says, "Give me a minute."

People have spilled out to the roof and with them in the warmish fall night is another tall man, one who seems to be as tall as Magnus. They're backlit so I can't see their faces, just the silhouettes of two fit, lean men. And they're arguing. Pointing. I start going towards them, because I don't know why. I just want to help. And I want to be close, and even though it's wrong, I want to feel the magic of his touch, or even just his presence.

But when I reach him, he drags me off to the stairs and away from whoever he's talking to. I'm hustled down first, Magnus at my back as the voice follows. "No, honest. Real nice talk, Mag. Loved it. Do it again soon?"

"Asshole," he says.

We hit the kitchen and he takes my hand, pulling me past Suzanne who says, "Go girl!" And gives me the thumbs up.

It's not until we're on the street and cutting through the park that I get my mind back into reality. "Magnus."

I pull free and stop.

He turns.

"What was that?"

A muscle in his jaw works and a thousand different expressions flit over his face. "Someone I didn't want to see."

"It sounded like he knew you."

For a moment I don't think he's going to answer, but a buzzing sound comes from the back pocket of his jeans and he pulls out the latest smartphone that's just hit the market. I know that's what it is, because Suzanne has been coveting it since before the release of the quad digit device.

He grimaces and slides it away. "Leftover perk from my old job," he says by way of explanation, and my cheeks go up in burning flames.

"I—I wasn't judging. Or asking."

"I should sell it."

Then he gives me a small smile that doesn't reach his eyes. "That guy was someone I know, yeah. A pain in the ass."

"Someone you worked for." Oh, God. What if the man was the reason Magnus no longer has his money making job? What if it's not just he quit, but he got forced out?

"Something like that. I'll take you home, Zoey. I need to stop by my gran's."

"I've love to meet her."

He starts off across the park, towards the Lower East Side end of it, and I hurry to catch him. After a moment he slows a little, and then when we hit the sidewalk, he hails a cab and I immediately scrounge in my pocket for my wallet because he's got enough to deal with and I don't pay him enough.

"No—"

"You work for me, I made you come out. So I'll pay for it." I can make the twenty plus bucks somehow work with my stretched budget.

We head to toward Delancey Street and the Williamsburg Bridge.

He doesn't say much. Just sends some texts.

I glance at him then watch the stores and streets pass as we drive down Broadway and finally turn off onto my stretch. "Your gran's pretty savvy with text."

"She is." And when we pull up, he looks at me, his gaze dropping to my mouth and deep down inside me things begin to tingle. "Thanks, Zoey, for taking me out. It was good. We should do it again."

I lick my lips and he takes in that motion with dark onyx eyes and it's only my sheer stubborn will that keeps me from launching myself into his arms and ravishing him there and then. Well, that and I'm his boss.

"I don't think it's a good idea."

"No," he says, "you're probably right."

"Goodnight, Magnus. I'll see you tomorrow."

"Tomorrow." I go to climb out and he says, "You know, maybe you should meet my gran at some point."

"I'd love that." And I rush up to the store and unlock the side door that takes me to my apartment. He stays until after I relock the door.

And it's only when I hear the cab pull away that I give in to the shake in my knees and sink down to the floor in the tiny foyer.

What the hell was that kiss?

Awkwardness seems to have become my middle name the next day.

At first, I don't think he's turning up. It's a little cool and the clouds are back and Tuesday Harry comes in, a big grin splitting his face. It's not Tuesday, but sometimes he likes to shake things up, plus I think he's got some secret inbuilt radar for when I make a spiced apple cinnamon sponge, and dark muscovado sugar cookies.

Those weren't my plan, but at four am when I woke, I knew I couldn't get back to sleep. I got up, drank hot chocolate mixed with fresh espresso because I like that sort of thing, and baked. Then I went over all the books, fretted about the payments for taxes and utilities, now I had a wage to pay. And then I fussed along the aisles. And waited for ten a.m.

It's almost eleven now. And there's no Magnus.

Maybe I'm a terrible kisser. Worse, maybe he somehow contacted Bronn and they both decided I'm a terrible kisser.

I'm being a maniac, I know that. I shove extra cookies and cake at Harry, who willingly eats them all up.

He shakes his plate in my direction, showering the floor with tiny crumbs. It's a good excuse to get the vacuum out later. I do my best soul decimating when I'm cleaning. "You look different, Zoey. Are you having a baby?"

I give him a mock-severe look. "Are you calling me fat?"

"Now, now, don't be like that. You know you're my favorite book girl," he says, winking.

"You think you're being charming, but you're not."

He chuckles and sets down the plate, eyeing the cake, and so I cut him another piece and give it to him. And my gaze wanders to the door that stays closed and Magnus free.

"I only mean you're glowing. And, I'm always charming."

"I think that's the accent."

"It's well known all Jamaicans are charming."

"You've been in New York how long?"

Harry starts counting on one hand. "Fifty-three years."

"You've been here since you were a kid."

He chuckles again and straightens his tie. And I duck behind the counter to get some of the books I put aside for him.

"Oh, Zoey girl, what are we going to do?"

"I'm not selling."

He sighs and I know what he's not saying.

"There's no way I'm going anywhere."

The bell tinkles and a cool breeze swirls in along with a wash of noise from the world beyond my store. For a moment, every nerve ending sings and trembles, but it's not Magnus. He'd say something, and he isn't the type to be so late. At least, I think he's not. "I'll be with you in a moment."

Harry leans over the counter and looks at me. "Did you meet a man?"

"I'm pretty sure that's the first question you should have asked."

"Yes, Zoey," says a rich, low voice, alive with warmth and humor, "did you?"

I surge to my feet, narrowly missing Harry and bashing my head on the side of the counter. For a moment, my ears ring and my heart goes wild.

"Magnus."

"You did meet a man!" Harry looks at him. "Did you—"

"Harry!" I'm not having him ask Magnus if he got me pregnant. "This is my new assistant."

"Magnus," says Magnus and holds out his hand.

Harry studies that hand like it's a fanged snake. "You sure he can handle this work? Have you seen those hands? I don't think he's done a day's hard labor in his life."

"You're a retired accountant, so neither have you."

Harry isn't bothered. "I've thought about it."

"This is a bookstore. The heaviest labor is shifting a box of books."

"Well, what about when you two—"

"Harry! There's a whole new shipment of knitting books."

Harry sniffs. "I'll have a look."

"I didn't think you were coming," I say, my cheeks going nuclear hot the moment Harry lopes off toward the aisle with the knitting books.

"I should have called but..."

"Is it your gran?"

Harry is back. "Gran? Got a pic?"

I give him my best evil eye, but he just waves a hand in the air at me and returns to the aisle.

"Yeah. I'll...um...organize the books for you."

"They're out."

"I mean the ones we didn't unbox."

There are boxes of them that I'm not yet sure to do with on the third floor, but maybe if he does that, I can take care of things here and not have to redo whatever he does to my poor register. I smile brightly. Really, what I want to do is bury my face against his chest and breathe that scent of his down into my lungs. And maybe try the kissing that's never happening again, again.

"Third floor." I toss my keys to him. "You can't miss the boxes. Just...organize them into groups until you can't stand it anymore."

For a moment he looks like he's going to say something, but he just nods and turns and heads for the stairs.

And I tell myself I'm relieved.

"Tuesday Harry?" Magnus looks up at me from the aisle of books he's walking down and my heart gives a little thrill. "Also, knitting?"

I wave my hands in the air. "He says it keeps arthritis at bay. He also says the romance novels he buys keeps his mind active, but I think he misses his wife. She died five years ago and he took over buying the things she did. Mostly he just comes in and doesn't get books, but when he does, it's those on the whole."

"Gotcha."

"He'll occasionally pick up books he likes, too, racy thrillers and old school detective novels, but I think he really misses her. He asked more about your gran."

Suddenly a wave of anxiety washes down over me. "Is she okay?"

"It was a bad night. I really should have called and—"

"You can take off all the time you need," I say to him.

He hovers, then goes to make a coffee and I brace myself for calling in someone to fix it, but he makes two cups like a pro. He adds the sugar and the milk for me and gives me a piece of cake, even though I don't ask for any.

And he looks down into his little cup. "I bet you didn't charge him."

"I did."

But he laughs and shakes his head. "A dollar?"

My cheeks burn. "It's my store."

"You've a good heart, Zoey," he says, sounding a little sad. Then he looks at me, and says, "About last night..."

Oh. God.

# Chapter Nine

## MAGNUS

The look on Zoey's pretty face is priceless, like I'm about to press charges.

She doesn't want to talk about it and I really don't plan on doing that, but it's perfect, and I need her thinking this guy she's talking to, maybe developing soft feelings for, is sweet and worth her bleeding heart.

This morning I had so much fucking work I couldn't get here earlier than I could. Pretending to be wholesome and inept is harder than it looks.

There's a fundraiser tonight for the homeless and I'm holding it. Not me personally, but one of my subsidiaries. I don't want the Sinclair name on it. I want to show I can do virtuous things without putting my name up in lights. But maybe it's a good way to work on my plan of stealing everything from out beneath pretty Zoey's feet.

It's not stealing, I tell myself, because I'm planning on giving her an outrageous payout once I have this place. It's just the way I'm going to get it is a little...unconventional.

"I wanted to say thank you. It's been a while since I've been out and about, and..." I shrug and give her my most disarming smile, and sweet Zoey smiles back. "You work hard here, and I wouldn't ask, but..."

"Anything."

There it is again, that bleeding heart complex she has that seems to come with a touch of hero complex. It's like she never read one of these damn books. It's like she's not from this modern New York.

Actually, that's it. There's an air of…not old fashioned, but other world about her, like she's from a time when people left doors unlocked, and trusted without a second thought, and gave their coats to a stranger without question.

I make a note to check her locks in the evening. I'm basically teaching her about the world, which she needs. Sure, I have to trick her out of her building, but that's part of the lesson.

"I might ask for a million dollars." I come up to her, because she smells good and the scent is low, subtle, tantalizing, and needs a man to be up close to appreciate it. Something, I'm sure, to do with the heat of her body. I pick up one of her dark curls and twist it in my fingers.

Her breath is uneven and her pupils large as she looks up at me. And damn if that mouth of hers isn't soft and inviting. I bet it's better savored, tasted slow and deep. Last night wasn't anything, even if it did hit my cock with some kind of dark magic, that fleeting little kiss.

"I don't have a million dollars. But if I did and you needed it, I would."

She sucks in a breath and it's like time goes still.

All it would take is me to shift a little closer, stroke my thumb against her cheek, and brush her lips once more. She'd give everything I ask for with that kiss.

Inexplicably, a burst of anger heats my blood and I step back. How has she even survived so long being her?

But that's to my advantage. "I don't need a million bucks." And it's really true. I don't. "What I do need is company. Tomorrow night. For a good cause. A charity dear to my heart."

"I'll check my social calendar." She looks at the ceiling a moment. "I think I can squeeze you in."

Homeless events go on all the time and I'm aware there's a deeper problem at work than just throwing money at it, like feeding the world's starving. All things I'm…throwing money at. I do, anyway, but these are things my mother will see through. And I know that woman's got Jenson's ear. So I need to build on what I have, and this idea is going to take at least a day to throw something together.

"You didn't ask what it was."

She shrugs, and it's so disarming for a moment it's hard to breathe. "I don't have to. You're a good person, Magnus. Only a good person looks after their aged relative and gives up bigger opportunities."

"You'd do it."

"I..." Her gaze shifts.

"You have, haven't you?"

She nods and looks back at me with tears that shimmer but don't fall. "I know you don't understand how special this place is to me, but my grandparents...my grandpa worked the store. But my grandmother, she was the backbone. She sacrificed and fought off the wolves when they circled. And..." Zoey laughs. "It doesn't matter. Suffice to say, this place means the world to me, which is why no big corporation is getting their hands on it. Once I go, the whole neighborhood crumbles."

Which is the idea.

"It's for the elderly. Making sure they have enough, their dignity and as much freedom as possible." It's so perfect, I sigh. And I haven't even gotten to poor nonexistent gran's need for an operation, and the fact my evil company is going to turf her out unless she can come up with tons of cash.

Ignoring the twinge of guilt, which is probably lack of sleep and nothing more, I continue. Little nuggets doled out over time. Like fishing. Or what I imagine fishing to be like. I don't have time for such crap unless there's a huge payoff waiting for me at the end of the hook.

"With Gran..." I pause, giving her room to imagine everything she can. With Zoey's sweet nature and soft and giant heart, I'm sure she can go places my black heart doesn't know exists. Which is why it's perfect. "Her injury brought home just how important having freedom, being able to do things like eat, go to the bathroom, get around, and have a roof and a routine, is to someone's physical and mental health. Especially when they're older."

"I'll go." She catches hold of my hand and squeezes, and I feel it everywhere. "I'll bring my checkbook. Just let me know when and where."

"No, you don't make a donation."

"I have to...I want to."

I kiss her on the cheek. It's soft and warm and lovely and not enough. Dangerous. I don't even know where that word comes from, but it somehow fits. Touching her, kissing her, it's dangerous.

Because....

I don't know why.

I shove it away. "No, you being there is enough. And we'll go from here. Should we get back to work?"

"Yes. You're a good man, Magnus."

I'm exceptionally good at what I do, but I'm not a good man. I'm ruthless. Down to the marrow.

And I've hooked her.

Everything is going swimmingly. What could possibly go wrong?

"If you're going to give me a hard time, I'm going to kill you."

Ryder gives me a wounded look at the House the Homeless fundraiser as I sip my whiskey.

"I'm not the evil type. Bad boy in the bedroom department, sure. But evil? That's more you. Or King." He brightens. "I could seduce her. She'll sign over everything—"

"No." I shoot him my darkest look. Fuck that.

I want her building, not Zoey with a shattered heart over my fickle brother.

"Hmm."

"Don't hmm me."

"Who's hmming people?" Scarlett scurries up, her dark blonde hair pinned up on her head, looking curiously from me to Ryder.

I make a note to keep my brother's brand-new wife away from Zoey. Something tells me they'd like each other. And something else, like Scarlett's accidental penchant for talking too much, tells me it's an extra bad idea for them to meet. She'd probably tell Scarlett who I was and then game over.

The event is going nicely. Moira, the woman who handles my charity events, is one of the best. She's liaising with the right people and I've set up an intricate dance of keeping this out of the papers and news while also making sure it's leaked.

I'm building my heart, and I have four weeks to do it. But I've also got her working late setting up a grassroots style fundraiser for tomorrow, one that's silently backed by my company. No going through other holdings; I want it known that while I'm changing the landscape of New York, I'm also helping the people who built it.

It's enough to make my dead father rise from the grave to haunt me. And hopefully it's a big step in my four-week trek to show Jenson and his team I have enough heart to get the fucking stupid earrings and secure our ownership in father's company.

Our company.

The true legacy.

"Mag's got ideas," says Ryder, nabbing another champagne from a passing waiter. A string quartet plays Vivaldi. "But he's making me his big bad."

"What's this?" Hudson comes over and slides his arms about Scarlett. "Why?"

"The stupid letter."

"And you have to make Ryder the bad guy?"

"Take the money and run." Great. Now Kingston's rocked up. "It's all about the money here. We can do this bullshit. But those jewels are going to be worth something."

"Why can't it just be a romantic take on our legacy?"

"Romance makes zero. And I'm not interested in anything more than cold, hard cash. Speaking of, I've made a hefty donation. One that's going to do well on my tax returns."

And then he's off, checking his phone.

The others look at me. At least our mother isn't here. Yet. I sigh. "Look, I have to show I've got heart—" I ignore Ryder's laugh "—to get the earrings and do my part in keeping the flagship in our hands. And I need to get this woman, this thorn, out of the damn way so I can build."

"Yeah, and he's doing this by pretending to be a good guy, working for the bookshop lady and stealing it out from under her. And, he's making me the bad guy in this," Ryder says.

"You turned up at the party."

"He was going to kiss her."

"Part. Of. My. Plan." The kissing part wasn't, but it doesn't make a difference. Zoey's attracted, and yeah, okay, I'm attracted back, but that's what makes this work the way I'm playing it. I can play her.

"You took her to a party?" Scarlett's giving me that look that says she thinks she understands but doesn't.

"It's not his kind of party. I was there."

"Ry, that makes no sense. We attend lots of the same things."

"But you took a woman who's totally not your type."

Hudson glances at his wife. Honestly, he's gone soft. "That might go south in ways you don't get."

"Can we leave it?"

"No." Ryder sips his champagne. "I want to know why I'm the bad guy."

"Because I can't clone myself. And I just said I told her you were evil and I worked for you. That's all. It's not like I want you to waltz in and win some kind of acting award. I don't want you anywhere near her."

"Why not?" Scarlett asked.

"We look like brothers and he likes to do things that win him labels and infamy. She doesn't like billionaires—"

"She's worse than you. To you I'm evil, and now she hates me without meeting me." Ryder shakes his head. "You'll be needing to give me those earrings when you get them."

"I don't want earrings," I mutter. "They're really not my style."

"Don't knock it. Dangly jewels might look good on you."

Ryder's an idiot.

"Look, I'm doing this for all of us. Keep the family company in our hands. And I need her damn building gone so I can build my legacy. She won't hand it to Magnus Sinclair, but...maybe to a nice guy down on his luck, desperate for money to help his dear, imaginary gran. And I've got a plan."

"A gran and a plan?" asks Hudson.

"I'm playing the small guy. Zoey will see all the pressure I'm under and she'll hand over her business, thinking she's saving my fake gran and me."

I don't even know why I'm explaining this to them.

Scarlett frowns. "Are you sure this is the way forward, Magnus? Things have a way of biting you when you're not looking."

"Zoey..." I trail off. I almost say she doesn't have teeth, but that's not true. She's got more bite than people give her credit for. But she just doesn't use it in the ways others do. She uses her teeth for good.

My metaphors are all over the place and I have limited time to get things moving. "I'd love to say this has been a good talk, but...well...you know."

"Be careful, Magnus," Scarlett says softly.

I glare. "I have a meeting."

And with that, I head out and back to my office. I call Georgio and tell him to meet me. We're upping the game. Attacking on all fronts. Subtle and not subtle. I need to see her under fire. I need to see her with the pressure on. I need her defenses strained to the limit.

I need to make my move.

And my fucking family?

They're all totally wrong. Nothing's going to bite back. I'm going to get what I want. And Zoey...

She's unfortunately going to be another failed small business.

Nothing is going to go wrong.

At all.

# Chapter Ten

## ZOEY

It's not a date. That's my mantra and I need to stick to it.

So what if I picked out a pretty dress with dark blues and greens to wear today. So what if I managed to find my mascara and perhaps a little eyeliner and tinted lip gloss.

Sometimes, a girl just happens to want to put all that stuff on and feel pretty.

For no reason whatsoever.

And if Magnus Simpson makes my palms sweat and my heart think it's a jazz drummer performing a bebop solo, so what?

It doesn't mean anything.

Anyway, tonight is just a fundraiser, two colleagues going out to help others less fortunate. And that's a far way off.

But I feel good, light, even though the sky outside is gray and drizzly. I've already turned the sign to open. Early this morning I made German chocolate cake with a coffee and raspberry drizzle, and simple little white chocolate cookies with dark raw sugar, cacao butter and butter.

The bell tingles and I smile.

But that melts away to a frown at the sight of the small, severe man in a mac coat and natty suit. He has a clipboard and marches up.

"Miss Zoey Smith?"

"Yes?"

"John Rogan." He flashes an ID at me and my heart sinks down to the soles of my sensible heels. Health inspection for permits, food safety. I've heard the nightmares. Mrs. O'Malley loves to regale me with tales from the dark side that they'd had to go through with the bar.

I don't even know anyone from the mafia.

The man eyes the cake and cookies. "Permits? I got a tip off you were selling food made in your home. There are all kinds of violations and inspections needed. Not to mention licenses and certificates."

I'm not a liar, but I'm going to give it a good try, because I haven't put up any prices yet.

"I have cake and cookies if you'd like some..."

"A bribe?" His eyes narrow and I almost recoil.

"What? No. Me? Never." This is why I didn't want to be a lawyer. They're too slippery. I don't want to have his job, either. Too slimy. "I love baking and I like to give a little something to the neighborhood. For free." I lean in and lower my voice, even though it's still early and no one comes in yet.

Magnus isn't scheduled for another twenty minutes.

My stomach clenches in a different way at the thought.

"I have a sweet tooth, so it's mainly for me to munch on, but I don't mind giving a cookie to someone if they ask."

His eyes narrow into little slits and he writes something down. "And the coffee?"

With a sigh, I tell him the coffee is for me. And by the time he's done with the promise or threat he'll be back, my good mood is nothing but dust.

I clutch the sheet of paper he gave me and shove it under the register, just as a rumble of thunder rolls.

"Hey, you all right?"

Magnus is there and I jump at the smooth, low sound of his voice. All my pulse points are on fire. He must have come in just as the thunder sounded.

His hair is damp from the light drizzle and he looks dewy and gorgeous and almost enough to forget the inspector.

"Great. Everything's fine."

"You sure?" He searches my face. "Because you haven't offered me a cookie—"

"You never eat them!"

"—and you don't have the prices up."

I shrug. He's got enough going on, so I'm not going to burden him. "I give them away mostly, anyway, so why bother? Let's get going. The day isn't going to get any younger!"

When the mail comes that day, it seems all my bills are coming early. They're not, but it seems that way. I put them in a pile behind the counter to take them upstairs to deal with Sunday night.

At six, when he leaves to get me milk because Magnus seems to be a shining light in that drab day, I get a hand-delivered letter. It's not a letter, it's more like a fine to do with the sweets.

"This can't be normal!"

The bell dings and all my senses are on alert as I know Magnus comes in. A plastic jug of milk hits the counter and he takes the paper from me. He frowns. "What the hell?"

"They can't stop me giving things away."

"It says here sales—"

"I can read." I snatch it back and fold it up, and grab the milk and put it in the little fridge I have on the other side of the counter. "I'll pay it."

"It seems hefty."

"I'll be looking into it all," I say quietly. "But big money speaks. So I won't sell, I won't display them and that's that."

"Do you make revenue? I mean..."

I glare at Magnus, even though this isn't his fault. "They aren't really about making money, although a little here and there never hurts. It's about creating a cozy space, a neighborhood store where people can get books, and if I give them a treat, then maybe they'll buy more down the track, or they'll tell people."

"Or you feed someone."

He sort of looks at me like he's angry, but I must imagine it because that expression vanishes.

"This is about that....bastard...Edward Sinclair. He's trying to stronghold me out of this place. It's just another little thing in a long line of little things."

What Sinclair doesn't get is the harder he pushes and bullies, the deeper I'm digging in my heels. I might be seen as soft or nice, but I'm also more stubborn than a gnat. Little, but with persistent staying power.

"So, just sell."

"And give him something to drag me into some kind of war with the health department, or whoever he's paying?" I lift my chin. "Unless you mean here."

"What?" He's silent a split second. "No. I meant your little treat."

I rub a hand against my temple. "I just want it all to stop."

"Then how about that fundraiser, Zoey?"

He holds out his hand, and even though I know it's a bad idea, I put my hand in his. "Lead the way."

I look around. It's an old warehouse, near enough to Williamsburg, one that's nestled in amongst the religious statue stores and ice cream truck places, all the little things no one ever thinks about being an actual business or supplier. But around here are artist studios and rental spaces and old school bare bones boxing gyms.

The place is done up enough. There are drinks for sale and music and all kinds of people.

Magnus makes a donation at the front door. I don't see how much he puts in, but I make a note to do so when he's not looking.

Cool young things with money are here. The well-heeled too. And women basically drool and follow Magnus with libidos in their gazes as he treks to the drink table and back to me.

"They have red wine and white wine."

"White, please."

He smiles that slow smile and flashes his dimple and my knees go weak and wavery. "Here you go."

"There's a lot of people."

"I know. What's the use of having had a career in marketing if you don't put word out," he says.

"You?"

He shrugs. "It's close to my heart." Then he looks past me. "Is that...Tuesday Harry?"

"I invited some neighborhood people."

Harry's deep in conversation with a slender older woman who's very animated.

"You know what they say…great minds think alike. And thanks."

"Word gets out and it helps good causes." I glance about. "Do you know who's throwing this? It's…"

I trail off because there's something about his expression that sets an alarm bell off in me.

"What?"

"Don't worry about it." He slides his hand down to mine, but I reluctantly snatch it away.

"Oh, my God. This is that horrible man's charity, isn't it?"

Magnus turns a darker shade. "I don't know about that, but the bartender just told me they're having an art auction and there are a few Sinclair family pieces here. So I asked a few more questions and…he's put money in it. Maybe he's not that bad."

"He is." I want to go and I down half my drink. I'm being unreasonable. This is a good cause and I'm aware people like my ex, and more so, people like Edward Sinclair, are involved in everything and anything that can get them a tax break or a sympathetic public appearance. "Actually he's worse."

"Really?"

"Yes."

"How so?"

I down another big swallow of my drink and glare at Magnus. "Because it's all fake."

"But it's for a good cause."

I sigh, defeated. "I know, but he's causing a lot of these problems by trying to make everyone leave their homes on my block so he can add more millions to his billions to give people with lots of money a home they don't need."

"Billions to his billions," Magnus says, taking a sip of his wine.

"I think I should go home."

"No." He captures my hand and draws me close. Against my better judgement I let him. That thumb moves slow over my flesh and I'm quivering inside. "Stay. It is a good cause, Zoey."

He brushes up against me and my good sense and outrage give up and sizzle down into need.

"Magnus," I whisper, "I thought we agreed this was a bad idea."

"No one agreed anything. I work in a shop with you. Fire me. Then maybe I'll ask you out..." His mouth whispers against that sensitive spot under my ear and I moan a little. "Or maybe we can just be two adults, two colleagues who are having a fun evening for a good cause. I like you, Zoey, that's all."

My head is spinning. "Magnus—"

"You know what this place needs?" Tuesday Harry says, grinning at us, ruining the moment, saving me from a mistake.

Me and men...I make mistakes. And all my energy is tied up in saving my home, my heritage, my neighborhood.

I smile at Harry. "Do I want to know?"

"A roller disco. All the kids are into it. There's one in Bed Stuy, just off New York Avenue that's old school cool. Back in the day, I could really do some roller moves. Got me all the ladies..." He mimes swishing around. Then he gives Magnus a hopeful look. "Is your gran here? I was talking to the organizer. There's some real money here tonight, and every cent made is going to build a center and help set up dignity services for the old people."

He says this like he isn't one.

"How is your dear grandmother?"

"She's home with a care giver tonight. Someone comes in once a week. I'd...she has a bad hip."

"Surgery?"

"Harry!" I almost groan. Next he'll be asking for her phone number. But he spies an old lady with green hair and pearls and makes a beeline for her. "I'm sorry, it's not his business. And—"

"I like him," Magnus says, humor lacing his words, and there's a part of me I didn't know was tense that relaxes. If he likes Harry, then all is good.

And secretly, I want to ask the same question Harry did, but for different reasons. I think, though, Magnus will talk about it when and if he wants to. It's not my business until it is. Still...

"He's lonely. You know you'll have to introduce him to your gran at some point."

"I just might." He's still got my hand and it feels right. "You know, you don't have to like this Edward—"

"Good. Because I don't."

"But you have to give it to him. He's doing a lot of good, showing heart."

"He's a cynical monster who's doing this for nefarious reasons."

I don't know this for sure, but it fits.

Anyone who kicks out poor people, old people and the lower working class for luxurious buildings and then has a charity to help is diabolical.

Magnus laughs softly and lifts my hand, brushing his lips against it. "You're one of a kind, Zoey."

Suddenly he goes stiff as a cloud of subtle, expensive perfume wafts over us and an elegant voice says, "Magnus? Aren't you going to introduce your friend to your mother?"

# Chapter Eleven

## MAGNUS

Well, fuck. Of course my mother is here.

I smile at her and then at pretty little Zoey.

"If you'll excuse us," I say smoothly.

Then before either she or my mother can speak, I grab the perfumed, Dior-clad Sinclair Queen and steer her away by the elbow.

"What are you doing here, Faye?"

My mother offers a cool smile, one guaranteed to set my temper boiling and she knows it. "Can't a mother take an interest in her child's fundraising? Two in one week. I'm very impressed. But Magnus, dear, you know it's going to take more than a few charities to show you have heart. And who is that? Not your usual icy sex-pot types."

"Can one be both ice and hot?"

"She looks human."

"You're a real laugh, ma."

Her eyes narrow. "What are you up to? You have three weeks left."

"I know exactly how much time I have and just leave Zoey out of it, okay?"

"Zoey." My mother says the name like she's tasting it. "She looks not only human, but someone who could have those earrings in minutes, if you get my drift."

I do and I'm getting really pissed off. Actually, I'm pissed off at a lot. My mother for elbowing in and attempting her version of matchmaking. My dead father for this bullshit. Zoey for not selling like a good girl. And Zoey again, for making me like her and respect her.

Being at my own charity crap, even if the charity people don't know it, is pathetic. It makes me look like I'm doing exactly what I'm doing.

"Look, Zoey—"

"Pretty name for a pretty woman."

I resist the urge to swear. "Listen, leave her alone." I take a breath. This shit is getting more complicated by the second. "She's another charity. I'm helping her, but the catch is she doesn't know who I am."

My mother just looks at me, her expression giving nothing away. "You like her."

"Not like that."

"Like what?"

"You know what."

"Hmmm...."

People need to stop fucking saying that to me. "Catch is, she doesn't know who I am and wouldn't accept my help if she did." The help being me saving her from a life of barely scraping by. Putting it like that. I'm a saint. "She doesn't like our kind."

"People?"

"Rich people."

She's about to say something, but changes her mind. "Good luck, Magnus, but this isn't as easy as you think it is."

And then, before I can ask her what the hell that means, she turns and breezes off.

I go to return to Zoey and honestly, I don't want to be here anymore. Where the hell is she?

With a groan, I spot her. She's talking to the staff, and I find myself watching her as she flits about, making small talk to different people, pointing at the art, and as I sidle up, she's talking to someone who's clearly old, old money and telling them how fabulous this all is and how the art is an absolute steal at three times the price and how it's also not only helping the less fortunate but a tax write off.

And, against my will, I find myself smiling. Zoey is just so Zoey. She's sweet, she's smart, she's pushy without people knowing it, and I'm pretty fucking sure she's just made that old woman part with a huge amount of money.

When she turns, I go to her. "Have you donated all your money yet?"

Her cheeks turn pink and I make another calculation in my head to give her extra when I get her building. I can afford it.

"You know, I think I'm ready to go. Unless you want to introduce me to your mother?"

I take her to a nearby Mexican diner. Over tostadas and fries and a couple of Tecate beers—which aren't bad for a non-beer drinker like me—I realize I'm having a good time.

Because of her.

Zoey.

She's funny, disarming, and she's been telling me colorful stories of growing up in her part of Bushwick.

Zoey dips a fry in hot sauce and frowns at me. "What?"

"Nothing at all. You. I like you, Zoey," I say quietly.

"I like you." And her smile is worth a million dollars. "So, what about you? What's your story?"

Fuck, I need to come up with something that she'd like. Because even without all the subterfuge and my ulterior motive, she doesn't want to hear about the rich kid who knows more about hard work and the ins and outs of board meetings, take overs, and running a business than he does about the playground and neighborhood hopscotch tournaments, like she had.

Because we went to boarding school, we learned about the business from the crib and fun was allotted on my father's terms. My mother's attempts weren't met with much luck. Fun was making money. Beating out others. One upping and being the best, the brightest, and the strongest where it counts. Power. Money. More.

Fun now is the same, but I've added sex with the right women because the wrong ones waste time.

I went to Harvard, but not like so many moneyed people do. I got in, like my brothers, through hard work and on our own merit, but I'm also aware we had the safety net of money. Our father wouldn't have saved us or boosted us up, but we had money. And Zoey...she went to college, owes tuition fees, even with a scholarship she got—she didn't tell me this, I went over her finances. It was a good school, here in New York, but she attended parties, had a boyfriend, probably boyfriends, and wouldn't see my world as something good.

Even without her experience with Bronn, I can't ever seeing her wanting what I do.

Which is good. It's fine. This is nothing more than a game, no matter how much I find myself liking her.

This is also business. And business is cutthroat. Dog eat dog and whatever other cliché you want to throw and have stick.

It's why I'll always be rich and Zoey will always scrape by.

She's collateral damage and nothing more.

Pretty as she is.

"Magnus?"

"Sorry, just thinking about my gran." I'm beginning to sound like the worst sort of sap out there. A mama's boy, or in this case, grandmama's boy.

Which, I remind myself, she loves.

"She'd like you," I say.

"You know, I'm not trying to pry, but if your mom is here, can she help out?"

"My life isn't like yours," I say, skirting along the truth. "Mom's not the kind of person to do that. And she's heading out of town."

"Why was she there? Did you invite her tonight?" She blushes hard when I take my time answering. "It's not my business."

Zoey takes a swallow of her beer.

"Hey, ask." Because if I was the Magnus she likes, not the bastard she hates, then I'd tell her all about my mother. Who is actually a good person. "My parents split up when I was young and she drops in to see gran—dad's mom—when she can. She told me about the event, actually. I thought she was heading out of town. Ready?"

She nods.

"I'll walk you home."

It's not drizzling anymore as we make our way through the streets. People are about. Young thugs hang on street corners and drink from brown paper bags. But weirdly, many of them nod at Zoey.

I don't even know why I'm saying weirdly. It's Zoey. She's no doubt made friends with the local serial killer.

I take her hand as we walk because Magnus Simpson would, and I like the feel of her fingers wrapped about mine, the warmth of her flowing into me. The sweetness of the connection.

At her door, I stop and before I can think, I cup her face with my free hand. "I had fun. Again."

"That's me. Fun."

"You are, Zoey," I say, suddenly meaning it. Her skin is soft, warm silk beneath my fingers and her eyes are big and vulnerable. "Don't think that's not something special, because it is. You're smart and funny and sweet."

"Are you quitting?"

She bites her lip, looking horrified, and I laugh. "No. I'm not that easy to get rid of. I'm just telling you the truth."

"You're a good friend a-and colleague."

But she wants more. That's there in her face. Most women I know would use that to play games, hide it if they thought it would get them what they wanted. But not Zoey. She wears her heart right there on her sleeve.

"We can be more," I murmur, brushing the side of her mouth with mine.

She sighs so soft it's like she's running her fingers down my naked flesh to whisper over my cock. "I think that's a bad idea."

"Yeah, but sometimes they can be really, really good."

I kiss her softly and she sways into me.

She tastes like spice and hops and the dark sweetness of her. "And sometimes it can be bad."

Her mouth seeks mine and she kisses me. Before she can draw back, I let go of her hand and slide my arm about her waist, pulling her into me. "Maybe I like bad."

She goes to answer and that's when I kiss her properly, taking full advantage of her parted lips and they open more for me. I slide my tongue into the heat and wetness and hers meets mine.

Heaven. That's the word. Heaven tinged with dark fantasy and X-rated images that tumble into me.

I kiss her deeply, pushing her hair from her face, and slanting my lips against hers, drinking down, and she melts, wrapping about me and the kiss takes on a life of its own. It has the sweetest claws that hook in such a way that makes my breath hitch, my cock hard and aching, and my heart beat fast.

She's fire in the blood. A slow burn that can turn into an inferno if she's treated right. And I want to treat her right.

I want to strip her down bare, down to the bone. I want to make her beg and moan and come so hard she's mine.

I want—

It doesn't matter what I want. I stop kissing her, coming back in to bite her lip, lick the spot and brush her mouth with mine before I untangle us.

If I don't go, I'm not going to. Because I'm hot for her. Attracted. And I need to sort that, be in the right place. The attraction, that's a game I can play. I can do that. Use that. All's fair in the cutthroat world I live in. And Zoey...she's completely delicious.

"I should go. I'll see you Monday."

"I...yes...I..." She stumbles back into her door, and before I can think, I follow, crowding into her and taking her mouth again.

This time it's slow, I take my time. It's a waltz of a kiss, a violin of tender passion infused melody, and I kiss her throat, her nose, her forehead.

"Goodnight, sweet Zoey."

And then I step back, three times, until I'm at the curb. I have to. If I don't, I'll be in her bed or fucking her on the stairs. And that isn't for tonight. I need to get my own shit together. I need to wait and play the game when the timing is perfect. I wait for her to unlock her door and go inside.

Zoey's about to close the door when she says, "Magnus?"

"Yeah?"

"I'd love to meet your gran."

Her door closes.

Welp, as the kids say, I'm going to have to find myself a gran.

# Chapter Twelve

## ZOEY

I wake up Sunday morning buzzing.

That kiss...

Every time I close my eyes, I can feel his mouth on mine and the way my stomach flipped, the way the earth actually seemed to move under my feet.

It's a cliché, I know, but that's what it felt like; the earth moving like everything shifted under the power of that kiss.

Because it was powerful. It zoomed through me, awakening things I didn't know existed in me, like a small fire of desire burned everywhere. I've been attracted to men before, but this...oh, this. Everything else I've ever experienced paled in comparison to this. Every little moment in the past when I thought I was in love crumbled to dust.

Not that this is love.

This is plain old desire.

On the level I've never experienced before. And I'm...I'm in trouble.

It's not even that he works for me. It's just a job in a bookshop. It's me feeling like this. I understand all the love songs I've ever scoffed at. I'm floating.

Everything has an extra kick to it. Colors are richer. Things brighter. Like they are just before rain. But so much more.

Slowly, I get up and go through all the motions. Breakfast, coffee, shower. Accounting.

And that's the problem.

I'm flying high and I can't concentrate.

"Damn it." I can't let it happen again. I know that. He knows that. Maybe I imagined it.

I didn't.

Finally, I throw down my pen and pour a coffee and go and sit by the window on my sofa, staring out at the gray that seems to be a permanent fixture right now. Like an ominous warning.

Problem is, I think I'm waiting for the other shoe to fall from the heavens and hit me on the head. Hot men don't waltz into my life like this. They don't kiss me. And... maybe it goes all the way back to Bronn. Or maybe I'm just weirded out by the sweetness he fills me with.

"And maybe you're just looking for trouble. It was one kiss."

It'll probably never happen again.

Or maybe I can learn to enjoy good things like that kiss. Good things like Magnus.

And not overthink it.

Like Suzanna says.

With that in my head and my new mantra of the day, I buckle down to work.

It's five pm, almost on the dot, when the lights go out.

At six, I'm surrounded by hastily dug out ancient lanterns and candles.

By seven, I admit defeat.

It's not a circuit. There's no big outage, it's me.

And one thought comes to mind.

That evil bastard, Edward Sinclair.

Monday morning and nothing has improved. If anything, it's worse. I text Magnus and tell him to take the day off, with pay. After all, it's not his fault I can't open a dark store.

And now I know why.

There's drilling and banging and trucks. And a giant hole in the ground two doors down outside a boarded-up building.

They're not city workers. And at some point all around there are stickered signs stating work permits. And a notice on my door about the power.

I'm so angry. And I grow more and more furious as the day goes on. Because those lights aren't coming on anytime soon.

I'm furious, and I want to cry.

I don't. Instead, I start digging into everything.

I'm in deep when I realize the noise I hear isn't the noise from all the work, but someone banging on the door. I lift my head.

Magnus.

The sheer relief that sweeps through me is something I can taste as I rise from the stool behind the counter in the shop.

He frowns when I open the door, looking around. "What the fuck is going on?"

"Edward Sinclair." I gesture for him to come in.

There's a moment, small and electrifying, as Magnus meets my gaze and slips past me, his body almost brushing mine, and little ripples of awareness spread out over my skin. "What's he done now?"

His words warm me because it's like I've somehow found an ally, and I bite down on my burgeoning smile. Even with the stress I'm feeling, he lifts me into a lighter place, even if it is a panacea of the temporary kind.

"What hasn't he done? And why are you here? Not that I'm complaining, but...there's not any work to do."

He smiles that slow panty melting smile and everything swoons. "Can't a man check on a pretty girl?"

"Magnus, we—"

"Why are the lights off? Did you not get I was coming?" He takes a look at my face and frowns. "Let me guess. Your billionaire nemesis?"

I push a hand through my hair and realize it's probably resembling a fright wig, what with all the worrying I've done to it with my fingers, and...I don't know why it matters, but it does. The kiss still sings in my veins. A kiss that I can't let happen again. A kiss I want to repeat with the kind of desperation that rips through veins.

"There's construction, as you noticed, by him. I saw the signs."

Magnus frowns and heads to the counter. I follow. "Doesn't he own a lot of the block?"

"Yes, but not all. Not yet."

"If it's illegal, then do something."

"He's a billionaire, so even if it was, how am I going to compete there? I can't afford to take him to court or anything like that. Not with time and certainly not with money. The fact is, he can't go through with his plans if I don't sell. Keep it simple, right?"

"Right." He looks at me, those dark eyes electrifying. "But your lights?"

"I called the power company, and they said everything is working fine. So it's got to be somehow to do with them."

"You should have told me earlier—"

"I don't go running to people." I shake my head. "I'm not a weak little damsel. And there's nothing you can do or could do."

He steps closer to me. "Except keep you company."

"I'm not asking you to give up time."

"I wasn't aware that's what I suggested. Maybe I want to be with you. And, how about we look at the bright side," he says, his voice sending waves of desire through me, "this might be perfect for a candlelight dinner?"

I'm weak. But I know what he's saying.

I go to explain it's all wrong and we're not like that and we can't be like that, I do, when he holds up a plastic bag.

"Indian?" I ask, sniffing the air.

He nods and I might be in love with him.

Somehow, he's figured out my weakness for spice—especially Indian food. Sugar and spice. I'm a cliché.

And it's not love. I'm just hungry. Not to mention exhaustion and stress. Magnus sets the bag on the counter and comes up to me, his hands on my shoulders and he massages a little. It's pure heaven. He's worth his weight in gold with a touch like that.

"Hey, it's gonna be okay."

"I just...if this keeps going, how am I going to operate?" But before he can say a word, I add, "Don't worry. Your job, such as it is, is fine. Safe. I'm not selling, I'm not closing down. I own the building, after all. And if my grandmother could keep this place going, and hers before that, then..." I find a smile. "I can, too. It's easier to fight fat, corrupt wolves when you own the place."

For a long moment, Magnus doesn't say anything. But finally he nods. "Dinner?"

"Yes, please."

I lead him upstairs, and it's natural his hand is in mine as the stairs are down now, and I have the flashlight. I stop at the kitchen and grab wine, mugs, bowls, and cutlery that he eases away from me.

Magnus goes to set up at the kitchen table when I shake my head.

"I want to show you something."

His eyebrow rises and my cheeks burn.

"This way."

I lead him out of the kitchen and down the narrow hall to the back of the apartment. I live on the top floor, but there's a small staircase, so I lead him there. Up the narrow, steep steps and unbolt the door.

A gust of air hits as we emerge, and around us the lights of the city sparkle like their own kind of night sky.

Magnus stands perfectly still, a small smile slowly emerging, and he looks about. "Wow."

"Way back, people who lived here, my relatives and their tenants—the floors below my apartment were also apartments."

"The top level of the store and your storage?"

I nod and lead him to a table and chairs I've got set up. "Yes." I start putting things out as he hands them to me and we work together, like an oiled machine. "They used this space for growing food, washing, and the rest. I don't grow food, but..."

"You have a garden in the sky."

I laugh. "It's not like some of those curated ones rich people have, but it's my little slice. All though the neighborhood people would find spots to make their own, to make their lives better. This is one of them. And...I don't come up here enough."

He takes his plate, chicken chettinad by the look and smell. I don't know where he went, but this food smells divine. "You should."

"There are lots of things I should do."

Magnus takes a sip of his wine and leans back, looking so big and there and at ease. "You never talk about your family that much."

"Neither do you."

He sighs. "Tonight my mother was with gran before she leaves town." He rubs a hand over the back of his neck. "A cruise."

"She doesn't seem like the cruise type, unless you mean your gran."

"You'd be surprised." He looks down into his cup, and drops the other hand to his lap, the food still sitting in front of him. "Gran...we're fighting a battle, y'know? Like everyone."

"I know." I smile. "Life is hard, but sometimes it's finding the little things to be grateful for."

"Like you?"

Heat burns my cheeks and I laugh, shaking my head. "No."

"What did you do at school?"

"This and that. But I found this is the life I wanted, surrounded by books, baking, just bringing things to people in the form of escape in the pages of whatever story or thing they want. There are worlds down there. Entire experiences." I point down as if I'm showing him the store. "And you can run away, you can live another life. Or you can learn, gain skills, languages, or even just fall into the past."

"You're pretty amazing."

From below comes a screech of brakes, followed by animated and colorful shouting. We look at each other and start laughing.

After that we just talk and eat and drink. Subjects wind all over the place from me to...me, to this little part of Brooklyn. When I ask him questions, the answers are generic, and I wonder if he was hurt in the past or is embarrassed by having to work here. He's not the best worker, but I don't think it's that.

But I leave it because people talk on their own terms and pushing doesn't help.

Magnus is sweet and kind with an interesting hard edge. There's a touch of cynicism about him, too, but I put it down from working in what was previously a high-pressure job.

"What are you thinking about?" He packs up the stuff as the air turns cool. He's seen me shiver, I realize. "You went all quiet."

"How you don't really talk about you."

He shrugs and says, "I find you more interesting, Zoey."

"I'm really not."

"Actually, you really are. But let's get inside where it's warmer."

I groan. "And dark."

But I lead the way and once in the kitchen I light a lantern. The living room glows with light from the street lamps and buildings across the street, and I turn to say goodnight, determined to nip this whatever it is between us in the bud, when Magnus holds up the bottle. "Another glass? Then I'll get out of your hair. Work tomorrow."

"Wine sounds good because if this keeps going, then—"

"We make calls and sort it out."

I breathe out. "You're right."

Leading him down the short hall, I set my mug on the low coffee table and Magnus does the same, the bottle and his own cup.

And then he turns to me. His long fingers, warm and gentle, stroke against my cheek and I'm immediately in freefall. "I'll get to the bottom of this, Zoey."

"How?"

"Make some calls. I don't know. I know I don't like seeing you upset."

Before I can say a word, he drops his mouth to mine and kisses me.

I'm gone. I'm caught up in the kiss, the feel of his tongue, the heat of his mouth. His arms come around me and I'm lost. Completely, utterly, awash on a sea of sensations I want to drown in.

The kiss twists and deepens and need spikes, a throb that's physical, through my blood, my bones, my sinew.

I'm vaguely aware we're moving and I'm on the sofa, Magnus on me, his hard body so delicious I can't get enough.

He's heavy and his thigh slides between mine as he bites my bottom lip, sending a cascade of heat showering in me. He moves his mouth, biting, kissing, licking, sucking, along my jawline and up to my ear.

His hot breath and gentle tug on my ear lobe sends me flying, the throb in me, deep down in my center, a physical thing and I bury my hands in his hair. It's thick and soft and delicious against my fingers and I pull him into me, needing more.

Down he moves, lower, along my throat until he bites down and sucks on my throbbing jugular and I almost come then and there. He's hard against me.

I can feel his erection. Big, thick, impressive, and I know I'm wet. I'm aching. I need. I need everything.

I haven't ever felt such a flood of emotions, of urges, of response to someone like I do him.

Not even as a teen with my first fumbling boyfriend.

Nothing compares to the dexterous melody he plays on my skin. I arch against him as his hands slide down my belly, and down over the front of my yoga pants. Shit, I didn't even think about what I'm wearing, but it doesn't matter because oh, God, it's like he's touching my bare flesh, his heat penetrating through the thin layers of the material and my panties.

Then his mouth is back on mine and I kiss him hungrily, urging him closer even as I keep my hands above the waist.

If I touch him, I'm completely gone. I'll let him do anything.

As it is, he's totally wrecking me, and I'm shaking as those clever fingers slide up, then beneath the elastic of my pants, and then down, into my panties and along the slickness of my pussy.

I hiss a breath as his fingers move back and forth and I arch up into him, wanting, needing...oh, yes... He circles his thumb on my clit and pushes one finger into me and my entire being rushes down to that place between my thighs and—

"Stop."

Magnus lifts his head, breathing hard against me, his finger still in me, and my body gives a little involuntary shudder, like the smallest orgasm. "Stop?"

"No...yes. Magnus. Yes, we have to stop."

Slowly he removes his hand and he buries his face in my throat a moment. Then he kisses my lips and sits up, smoothing my top back into place. "I... Sorry, I got carried away."

I don't even have to guess that he never has to say such things to females. Most would already be naked and on him. Most of those already wanting him as theirs. And me...

Shakily, I sit up, breathing out. "I...no, it's me. Magnus. I obviously like you, but I'm not a casual girl. I don't...I mean, I do. But not for a while." I bury my face in my hands and it's on fire.

"I get it. I should go. And Zoey?"

"Yeah?"

"Look at me."

I do, and I'm not sure I understand the expression on his face. It's almost like wonder mixed with need, regret, and faint surprise.

"Looking," I say."

His mouth lifts at a corner. "I really like you, too. This...none of this with you and me has any intentions other than what it is. I want you to know that."

I nod, not sure I understand the fullness of what he's saying because there are layers there, so many and I don't know where to begin or even if I should. "I do, but...we need to take this slow, or not at all."

Magnus looks at me for a long time. Then he gets to his feet. "Goodnight, Zoey."

And he leaves, and all I can do is sit there, staring after him.

# Chapter Thirteen

## MAGNUS

Three hours after leaving Brooklyn, I sit in my penthouse, looking out over the river and the nearby Woolworths building.

That...what happened tonight in her living room, the small slice of unexpected heaven, wasn't in the script. At all.

I put my bare feet up on my desk. The floor to ceiling window in my library/study and its view usually bring me focus and peace.

Not tonight. Tonight I'm...shit. I shouldn't have kissed her again. No...no, kissing her was something I'd planned, but the rest of it? That came from nowhere. It blazed in, overtook, and she was utterly delightful.

I want to fuck her. I want to bury myself so deep inside her I don't know where she ends and I begin. I want to pound her so hard. I'm over this fever that burns in my veins when I'm that little bit too close to her.

Jesus. She tastes like sin and all the sweet things the world has to offer.

Tapping my hand against my thigh, I force myself to go over everything once more. Already things aren't following my plan. I wanted her power out for a day. But...yeah. When I woke up my person in charge of all that, all I got was a story about how the systems are antiquated and the city hadn't yet come in to fix the power grid in that part of Brooklyn, to bring it all kicking and screaming into the 21$^{st}$ C.

I reamed out Georgio for good measure, although he sounded a little hurt and said he'd get on things for me. So I'm waiting for his call. And in my head, I can hear my brothers laughing at me.

Because I'm feeling bad about this plan.

But a few unasked for emotions aren't getting in my way.

And I can fix this whole thing. I want her pushed to a limit, to see how she takes things, but it's not the right approach. Zoey Smith is made differently. She'll sit there, and she won't budge. Even if I pay the entirety of New York to rain misfortune down on her, she won't give up.

Georgio calls me back. "We'll need a day. It was all ready for the city to fix the power grid, but since we're redoing everything with state of the art, we have special permits, and..."

"Fine. I'm putting you in charge of overseeing it tomorrow."

"Me?" Georgio takes a moment. "Boss, that's not the work I do."

"It is now. Make sure the guys on the ground have her power up and running tomorrow."

"Sure. And the other work?"

Thing is, I sanctioned this work, even though all the paperwork isn't signed for other parts of the block—people and places I'm not worried about. They'll come around. It's Zoey. Even though I now own most of the large block, her being the hold out means my plans will eventually slam into her. It's easier to have her gone than fight her in court.

"We need to get a start. Everything goes ahead. Just bring the lights back. She won't budge that way."

"I told you she's cray-cray. I bet you she'd sit in the dark for the next ten years than sell."

"Everyone has their point of breaking. I'm finding hers. Just make sure this goes the way I need."

"Yes, boss."

I ignore the large twinge of guilt. It's probably from the Indian we ate earlier. And it's probably indigestion. I hang up the phone and grab my laptop. It's time to see about Zoey's special breaking point.

I pull up the special account I made and click on the emails.

I almost laugh. Tons of responses to my ad I put up.

Looks like I'll be interviewing tomorrow for a gran.

And then I'm going to move in for the kill.

Combine the fruition of my ambitions with the next blast of fucking heart I'm ready to unleash, I'm on my way to winning big.

And Zoey…

I refuse to think any more about her for the rest of the evening.

"Hey, Zoey," I say the next morning, answering the call I've been expecting. "I'm on my way."

"Don't come in today. Still no lights." She gives a hysterical little laugh that cuts more than it has any right to.

"Are you sure? I'm going to make some calls for you. I was planning to do them at lunch—"

"No, no, I don't want you to waste your time. Spend the day with your gran."

I smile and pour another coffee, plucking out some blueberries from the container that sits on my pristine marble kitchen island. "Are you sure?"

"I'll pay you, so don't worry about that."

Jesus fucking Christ. This woman.

It's going to be a hard lesson she'll be learning, but one she needs. After all, no one can go through life being as nice and sweet as her without expecting to be burned. And she's going to get burned.

"If you're sure," I say.

"Yes, now say hi to your gran."

"That I will. That I will."

And I hang up and down my coffee, following it with the blueberries.

I'll make more than sure to say hello to the winning gran candidate.

Wednesday and Thursday I'm still interviewing, but after work—work, I'm fucking calling it work now—I hurry away from sweet Zoey. They're almost finished with the work on her street I sanctioned, but I quietly pay extra for them to work in shifts to have it done.

It's because it's giving me a fucking headache and not because I can't stand the look on Zoey's face, the toll it's having on her. No, it's got nothing to do with that.

I'm running out of time and I don't need my brothers to tell me that when we have a late meeting Thursday. They're worried about the flagship company, and to be fair, I am too.

We don't trust whatever the fuck our dead father is up to.

"It's worth a shit ton of money. And reputation." Kingston stretches out in my living room, a whiskey in one hand as he scrolls through his phone. No doubt he's got an eye on some new investments. I know how he is when that happens.

"I care about the heritage." For all his lazy air, Ryder, who's pouring a drink, dressed in his East Village vibe outfit, along with his reputation as a lady's man, works hard. And he loves the original company.

He looks around.

"And the money."

"We all have enough." Hudson is sending a text and it'll be to Scarlett. No one will color me surprised if they announce a baby's imminent arrival in the next year.

"It's not about that, Hud," I say. "It's about principle. We're being fucked with, manipulated from beyond the grave, and it's annoying."

"And we don't know what's going to change next."

"Because," I say, nodding at Ry's words, "that's what he's done so far. And he had some game plan in mind with these fucking jewels."

"We stick together and we keep the company, and we take our share." Kingston looks up. "At least, that's my plan. These jewels are worth a lot in reputation alone. So we just do the bullshit—"

"The bullshit is getting in the way of my project."

King lifts a brow. "Or is that the girl?"

"I'm handling that. And I'm handling the heart crap."

And I really am. So many things set to go.

"We'll be calling you Mr. Bleeding Heart." Ryder chuckles into his drink.

A low smile hits Hudson's face. "Or Mr. Philanthropy."

"Hey, this is for you, jerks. I'm good as I am." Which is mostly true. I want the heritage to stay our heritage and not somehow fall completely into public hands. I've seen too many highly regarded businesses dragged down that way. Still...

"What's your next move?"

"Zoey's a lot tougher than she looks."

Hudson gives me a funny look as I say this. "I meant," he says quietly, "the proving you have heart thing."

Oh. Right.

I outline my next moves. When I get to the one about the reading center, Zoey wanders into my mind, infecting me with the unease I'm beginning to know well.

Guilt. That's what it is. Misguided, unwanted, unwarranted guilt. I squash it once more and will it to stay that way, but the woman has a way of somehow breathing life into my conscience and letting the guilt flare up.

Damn pretty, sweet Zoey.

I can't wait to be rid of her.

And I just hope that one day when my dream is built, I'll be able to believe that.

One day.

Amelia Johnson isn't exactly grandmother material when she sashays into my office. More Studio 54, Good Time Gal, and broad who intimately knows the block and has it exactly where she wants it. She has to be around seventy, and I'm ready to dismiss her when she leans over my desk and pins me down with a hard glare.

"Boy, I've been dealing with your type long before you were born."

I lean back and look at her. "Billionaires."

"Yup. And movie stars. Mobsters. All kinds. You have a job, you have the pay, and I can show you why I'm worth my weight in gold. Also, I don't have a pesky conscience."

I point at her. "Sick gran. Frail. But has life. And someone a bleeding heart wants to give her life and soul and building to save."

She smiles. "Bathroom?"

It's Thursday night and I have a reading center to open in the name of my actual maternal great grandmother. So I check my watch, straighten my tie, and point to the executive bathroom.

The woman who emerges looks old. Frail. Sweet. Amelia hasn't done much, her dark hair is pinned differently, old fashioned, and she's moving slower, like things hurt. But it's her aura.

Somehow, someway, she's captured the idea I've been struggling to build.

The woman might have a heart as black as mine.

She hobbles up and talks to me in a slightly quavery voice. I hold up a hand and offer her a cool smile.

"If you manage to help me part this woman from her building, then I'll pay you triple."

And with that, I shake her hand, wait until she goes, and grab my jacket.

If my stomach seems a little heavy, I ignore it and head out. I have an empire to build, family heirlooms to grab, and a legacy to secure for my brothers and myself.

I don't have time for Zoey or emotions.

Of any kind.

By Friday afternoon I'm quietly amazed at Zoey.

Not her sweet smiles, or the way she works way too hard for too little, but at how she cares. People come in, more than I saw in my first week, and they're all concerned about the handful of days her store stayed shut.

She's also very easy on the eye, and the tension between us grows more palpable by the passing hour, as it's done since that...session on her sofa.

Did we nearly fuck? Yeah. I'm aware of that, painfully. I need to do something about it, because me not having sex and being attracted to Zoey is a dangerous recipe, a disaster waiting to happen.

It's not I don't think I can handle it, sleeping with her, but I'm playing a game and I moved too soon and—shit. I don't know. I like her. That's the problem. Too much. That's the other problem.

I can use that, but I have to do it my way.

And I'm talking myself in circles.

Her frequent, long side glances with her emotions in her eyes are what I want. Add some heart to that and I can really manipulate her.

By seven, she breathes a sigh, turns the sign, and locks the door. Then she stands in the middle of the store and looks at me. It makes my heart thump hard.

"You don't have to stay so late."

"I know, I wanted to make up for me not coming in. You insist on paying—" something I actively feel terrible about, but then again, fools and their money...even though I don't think she's a fool "—so it's the least I could do."

She nods. And opens her mouth, a worried expression on her face.

So I step in, right up to her, and slide my hands along her shoulders. Christ, she feels good. "Gran's been asking about you."

"It's the cookies I send with you."

I go to say she's diabetic, but for some reason I stop myself. I've been giving her treats to my PA who I swear swoons every time. If I say something snarky, it would be like slapping Zoey and I don't hit women. Even metaphorically. Not like this, anyway. "She loves them. And she thinks you sound like a dream."

"That's so sweet."

I lift her chin with my fingers. Dark circles shadow her eyes, and her soft mouth is pale. "So are you, Zoey. I don't think I've ever met anyone quite like you."

The moment I say those words, I know they're true.

Sure, I'm taking away her rickety store. Sure, I know it's going to burn her. But it's true. And part of me wishes things were different. The other part wonders what the hell the suddenly sappy part has been drinking and I know I need to get out of there.

I have two weeks to deal with the whole heart bullshit, which I'm off to do again tonight. I'm setting up a job and shelter service. Not a halfway house, but it came about from listening to Zoey yesterday. She was talking about the problem of people who'd gotten themselves up from the gutters of society, and how for some it's hard to find work, and that means it's hard to find a home. And then she told me about programs for ex-cons and how restrictive some are.

So I'm going to set something up. Offer housing and set up different kinds of places where people can work. As well as a place away from the city where people can make and sell things like home goods. That one came from Tuesday Harry and his knitting.

It's not happening overnight. And it might all sink terribly. Tonight is dinner and drinks with others who I think will be on board.

People love good deeds and projects, and for once, even if it fails, I'm fine with backing this.

"Magnus..."

Her mouth is calling to me, but I reluctantly step back, releasing her. "Keep that thought, those words, whatever they are. I have to go. And who knows, maybe I can bring Gran this weekend."

And Zoey smiles.
It almost breaks my heart.
If I had one.

# Chapter Fourteen

## Zoey

I'm going to have to fire him.

It's not the bad job he does. It's him. I like him too much.

Suzanne gives me a look. "What's that face?"

"It's my face. I have it all the time." I take a sip of my Jack and Coke. Not my usual, but I need the sugar and the boozy courage.

It's Friday night and it's been a few hours since Magnus left and his sweet words reverberate in my head. Yep, I'm going to have to let the gorgeous hunk of a man go.

She sits in O'Reilly's like the place is ready to bite her, or give her some kind of infection, or the poor gene, as she once actually called not having money.

Honestly, if I didn't love her, I'm not sure we'd be friends.

And I'm going to have to tell her. Especially since she's asked about Magnus about ten times in the last hour.

It's starting to get a little rowdy in here, so I take a deep breath and say, "I think I'm going to fire him."

She blinks like I suggested burning down a roomful of the New Yorker, her favorite magazine. "But he's gorgeous."

"I know."

"You have lost your mind, woman."

I can feel my cheeks heat and her eyes narrow. I slurp my drink down and go to get another when her hand wraps, vice-like, around my wrist. And some band throbs out a song about love and booze and broken hearts over the top of the crowd.

"Oh. My. God."

I point to the ceiling. "What? I can't hear you. Mr. O'Reilly's playing his music too loud."

"You..." Now her eyes go wide. "Did you sleep with him?"

Anything I want to do with Magnus Simpson and that hard rock body and onyx eyes has nothing to do with sleep. "We kissed."

"Zoey! Are you firing him to have your wicked way? Because if you are, just keep him. Office affairs are all the rage."

"They are not." I breathe out, snatch back my wrist, and take a sip of the dregs of Jack and Coke and icy water. It's not very nice. "And no. I just..."

She pats a hand over my head, like I'm a pathetic stray. "Listen to me. He's not that idiot from school who crushed your heart."

"Bronn did not crush my heart."

"Your confidence, then. You can have a man and work with him and a business. Modern women sometimes have lovers all over the place."

Suzanna makes it sound like they grow on trees.

"I..." I slump down. "I'm worried I'm going to jump him. He's so..."

"Hot. Like melt your panties off as if they're ice cream on a hot New York pavement on a hundred and twenty summer day."

"I was going to say lovely, but he's got a sick gran and...also...I wouldn't put it that way, but yes."

"And you said he needs the money!"

She's got me. And I am scared. What if he's like Bronn? What if he hurts me? Which is stupid because though I don't know him, he's been nothing but sweet and nice, with little bits of spice that keep him really interesting. "I know."

"Did you kiss him or did he kiss you?"

"Which time?"

She gasps, looking utterly delighted, and claps her hands. "It was him."

"Look at me, and look at him."

"I'mma looking, girl, and I think he has good taste. You're no glamor queen, but you have substance. We could go do your hair, if you like, spruce up your wardrobe—"

"I thought you said he had good taste."

Suzanna's able to turn a maybe insult on a dime. "I did. I was just saying if you're worried, we can do that. But he likes you. It's a store. It doesn't matter."

Ugh...do men talk like this? But... "I'll sleep on it. Another round?"

She nods and hands me a twenty. It's Brooklyn, old school. People prefer cash. I weave my way to the bar and as I go, I know it's just fear. And if I don't do anything about it, if I sit him down and say we can't do anything, then it will all be okay. Right?

Right?

It's late for me when I roll the half block home. I've put Suzanna in a car service, and I'm ready to curl up in bed. My mind is soft and I almost have a buzz from the handful of drinks.

Someone is leaning against my door and my stomach somersaults as my heart tattoos against my ribs.

Magnus steals my breath. He's so beautiful.

And maybe that's the problem. He's beautiful and nice with a sick gran and he's someone I could develop real feelings for. If he wasn't quite so much of a cypher.

I stop.

Where the hell did that come from?

A cypher?

But it fits.

I don't really know him or much about him, only he's a fantasy man. He's polite and sweet and lovely and I don't know what dwells under all that surface stuff.

He's the perfect man. He really is.

And he likes me and—

"You know, Zoey, I couldn't get you out of my head all evening."

He's dressed in black from his boots to his jeans to his sweater and he's utterly devastating. And maybe it's because I'm just the right—or is that the wrong—side of tipsy, but he seems different somehow.

The shadows and light from the buildings and the street lamp throw his cheekbones into sharp relief, and there's an air of sardonicity about him that makes my heart beat even faster, my blood heat.

"I had a thing—"

"You didn't see your gran?"

"She went to bed early and I had to attend something, and you were in my fucking head." He stays leaning against the door and taps his temple with one long-fingered hand. "And I kept thinking I shouldn't like you. Zoey Smith is way too sweet. She eats a lot of sugar and I'm...I shouldn't be here."

"But you are."

Now he straightens and comes to me. "I am. Because you're in my head, Zoey. You're sweet and taste like stolen moments and hot sex."

I can't move. Never in my life has anyone said anything like this to me. I'm rooted down to the spot on the cracked pavement, and not even the swish of cars or the honks of horns or people shouting and laughing can penetrate the spell he's weaved.

This is no cypher.

This is Magnus.

And I want him.

Desperately.

It's like he reads my mind. He slides his hands through my hair and kisses me. Not like before. This is a hard kiss. This is sex. It's naked, hot, erotic, and I'm not thinking. I hit the door, his body crowding me and the word yes is the only one in my head.

I kiss him back like this is life itself and he's devouring me.

He tastes my throat in ravishing bites that make me ache down into my core. That sweet aching need that presses against me and I need him in me. I release the hold I have on him and fumble in my bag, but he takes my keys from my shaking fingers and jams them into the lock, kissing me all the while.

His tongue is hot and the dance is wild and I'm slowly self combusting. We barely get in the door and he kisses me all the way up the stairs, all of them, his hands on me. Under my shirt, touching my breasts, teasing my nipples and I can barely hold myself together to not maul him on the stairs.

Once we're inside my apartment, we're in the small hall and Magnus drops to his knees, tugging my jeans and panties down and then his mouth is there and I'm trapped, his mouth at my clit, his tongue laving against it, his hand coming around and sliding down past my ass, to trail along the slickness there.

"You're so fucking wet, Zoey." He looks up at me and his eyes glitter. I'm shaking. I don't know what's happening except I need this. I need him. This Magnus, the one who isn't sweet and nice, but raw and forceful with an erotic current that buzzes in my blood.

He pulls off my shoes and clothes and I'm naked and he's not and he uses one hand to push me back against the door and then he lifts my leg and throws it over his shoulder and he buries his face in my pussy, and I come. Just like that, I shake apart in an orgasm that leaves me weak and open and shocked.

But Magnus isn't done. He keeps going, stoking the fires, using his tongue and teeth and fingers to bring me right up to the edge and then, still holding me, he takes that leg in one hand, the other holding me against the door, and he rises up, my leg about his waist.

We stare at each other and he says, "Why do I think you don't get to come nearly enough? We need to fix that."

"Magnus, you and me, I...it's wrong."

"I know."

"We shouldn't."

"I agree."

"You better fuck me now."

"Try and stop me."

I reach for his jeans and I undo them, and push them and his boxer briefs down enough to free him.

He's gorgeous. Utterly. Big and thick and there for the taking. "I want..." I take a breath. "I want to taste you."

"Later."

And he kisses me, deep, rough kisses that rub me in all the right directions and he lifts me up and positions himself at my entrance. And he stops kissing me then. Magnus stares at me. We're eye to eye and then he pushes in and I cry out because he feels so damn good.

It's like everything I've ever needed, whether I knew it or not.

He starts to move. I meet him, thrust for thrust, my short nails digging into the skin of his upper arms, that hard, hot muscle. We slam together, my hips raising, thighs widening, like I need to fit more of him in me than is possible, and he moans, burying his face in my throat and starts to move harder and harder. Inside, the sweet hot pressure builds and I fly apart. I crash down over and over and over again and then he shudders, coming, too, and we stay like that for a long time.

Finally he lifts his head and I wait for him to say that was a mistake, or to apologize or something that makes me wish we hadn't done that. Not that I think anything could.

But he just looks at me and says, "That, Zoey, was a great starter. Ready for more?"

"Oh, God, yes."

Tomorrow. I can deal with the fallout tomorrow, but now? I want this slice of heaven. I want it desperately.

He kisses me soft and gentle and says, "Bedroom?"

"This way…"

# Chapter Fifteen

## MAGNUS

I should regret this, but I've had just enough to drink and the need for her is too strong, that I don't.

We're both naked and she's utterly glorious. If this is going to be it, I'm going to make it last.

I'm not being myself. Well, actually, I'm being more myself with her than I have been. I wanted something and I went for it. And that something was Zoey.

"You have beautiful breasts," I say. "They're the perfect size. They fit my hand."

I palm one and lean down, sliding my leg up to hold her thigh down on the bed, keeping her open for me. And then I suck on her other nipple, making her back arch and push her breast to me. I take that invitation.

Biting softly, just enough to make her moan and shift and try and lift up her hips, I move to the other, giving it the exact same treatment. "See?"

Her eyes are half closed, languid, and she watches me. "I think you're drunk."

"Tipsy, but I've been thinking about your breasts since right after I met you."

"You have not."

"I have. I try and keep it professional. Bookstore professional."

That elicits a small laugh from her. "You're different tonight."

"Bad or good?"

"I like it, but this..."

I kiss her softly, stopping her words. "This is tonight, Zoey. The world can wait."

I am being different. I'm being me. More me than I think I've been in a while. Because right now I'm not playing games. I'm diving into the moment with her, something I don't do. Or, something I don't do like this.

Not reckless, not with someone as soft and lovely like her.

Not with someone I'm going to—

I don't let myself finish that thought. Instead, I continue my exploration of her. And I slide my hand low, down over her ribs, over the soft swell of her tummy, and then down, through the strip of short curls to that hot, glistening prize there.

I'm rewarded with her gasp as I tease her clit, then lower, along those lips, and down and into the hot, tight depths of her with my fingers.

She's moaning now and the sound of her voice when she's turned on should be bottled and sold. It's glorious and hot as hell.

"Magnus! Oh, God, you're going to make me come again."

I smile and start to finger her slowly, in and out, keeping a steady stroke against her clit until she starts to ride the wave, until she begins to tighten, her thighs trying to bear down together.

But I don't let her. I just keep up my slow rhythm and I watch her.

She still watches me back, but this time she gasps, drawing her bottom lip between her teeth, and she slides her hand down my face.

I curl my fingers inside her, and begin to hit her G-spot.

She loses it, and comes on my hand, thrashing in the bed, gasping for air.

Watching Zoey orgasm is a sight to behold. I'm hard as fuck because it's one of the hottest things I've ever seen.

She's gasping, muttering nonsense words as I hit that spot again, massaging until she's hit with a bigger, harder wave. And she pushes at me, then pulls me down on her and I kiss her and kiss her. It's like I can't get enough of her delicious mouth, those kisses.

I take my hand slowly from her body, but she wraps around me, still kissing, and I can't stop either.

And then my sweet little Zoey does something incredible.

She pushes me hard. Down onto the bed on my back and she rises up over me. At first I think she's going to fuck me and I'm all for it. This is a night of passion for passion's sake. Something I started, right or wrong, and if she wants to ride me, I'm going to let her.

But she doesn't. Instead she slides down my body. Zoey touches, kisses, explores, and then she comes to my cock.

And she takes me in her mouth.

Oh, holy fuck.

I nearly bust one from her mouth on me. Her hot, greedy, sucking mouth. She licks and sucks, up to the head, her tongue running under the sensitive edge and I bury my fingers in her hair. And then she swallows me down. So deep she gags. And she does it all over again. Again and again, all the time her hand working my shaft and balls and I can't help it, I start to pull her from me and push her down instead. Not hard, but enough to let her know what I want and she goes willingly.

She works me like she's going for gold. And I fucking come in her mouth.

My entire body is flooded with pleasure and then I pull her off me up and into my arms and I smooth her hair back. "You're a fucking wonder, Zoey Smith."

I kiss her. Long and slow and deep.

And then, we start everything all over again.

There's a haze over me when I wake. Zoey is splayed over me, sleeping, and she makes little sighing noises as her hand curls against my chest.

I slept with her.

Not just the act of sex, but I fell asleep.

It's not I haven't gone and done that before. A good, hard, tension releasing fuck at the end of a grueling day or week or whatever happens to go on, can sometimes bring about enough relaxation I fall asleep. But I never spend the night. Not unless it's a night designed for hard core sex that keeps us back at it until the day breaks.

And hell yes, I could do that with Zoey, just keeping fucking her. But sleeping with her?

I could do that, too.

I did.

And the haze is from the sex and from sleep and her. Maybe it's been a while I've just fallen so deeply asleep. I don't know. Outside, the day is gray again, and soft rain patters down. I can see the ugly building tops, old signs from decades ago of businesses that no longer exist, faded and chipped old paint. But somehow it doesn't bother me as much as it normally does.

That kind of ugly doesn't fit my aesthetic for what I want to craft in my areas of New York, but framed with simple cream gauze curtains, and a walnut wood-slatted set of blinds that match the frame of Zoey's wide bed, and wide planked floorboards she must have once spent days sanding, staining and polishing, it has a softer, more romantic look. A framed photo of life.

Zoey stirs, and looks up through a curtain of tangled black curls, those violet eyes soft. "You're still here."

"It's hard to do the sneak of shame when you're being used as a pillow."

"Shame, huh?" She bites her lip and pokes me in the abs. "You're very...pillow-like."

I laugh, pushing away all thoughts except for her and here and my hardening cock. Flipping her, so she's under me, I nudge her thighs apart and she sighs.

Christ, I think I could spend forever with her.

The thought sits, and I poke at it, turning it to fit. This is how I need to be with her, to win her. I smooth the hair from her face, trying to make my brain get back to the mission at hand.

In a different world, maybe I'd wish for things I never think about. Maybe I'd wish for a chance to get to know Zoey as me. Or rather, have Zoey know me. But Zoey and Edward Magnus Sinclair would never mix, never be a thing.

I've no place for her world and she...Zoey wouldn't ever want me as part of hers.

But that's nothing but good sex and libido talking.

I don't have space for relationships of the kind Zoey would want in my life. And I like that. What she wants takes a different man. One way less self-focused than me. One with fewer ambitions.

Mission, I remind myself. I need to keep my eye on my purpose here.

"This is just for now, Magnus," she says softly, almost like she can read my mind.

"Is it?"

She nods, moving her hips up, like an unconscious offer of her delicious wares to me. "You don't talk much about yourself."

"What do you want to know?"

She sighs and moves again and I thrust against her because I can, because it turns her on, because I want to. "That's not why...I just...my life isn't yours, and my life is complicated right now. My energy is focused on keeping the store running, fighting off that billionaire bully..."

"Well...there's a thing called multitasking. Are you worried I'll up and leave?"

"I know you'll go back to your old life."

"That doesn't preclude you and me." What the actual fuck am I saying? The words come of their own free will. "I'm thirty-four. There's gran and making sure she's taken care of, and maybe one day I'll go back to my old career or maybe not. There are things I can do. It's a big world."

"And it's not all about money."

She's so wrong. "My life's boring. Or was."

"How so?"

"I got a job in a shop and got the hots for the quirky, pretty lady who owns it."

I slide my hand down along her hip, shifting her so my cock is right there, pushing at her entrance and she bites her lip. But I don't enter her.

I'm not sure who I'm torturing.

"Magnus..." She gasps, rocking up against me, but I hold her in place, a tease.

And I kiss the end of her nose, then her soft, plump lips and raise my head, staring into her eyes. "Things, Zoey, sometimes can just be."

And then I push into her, and I'm lost in her all over again.

That day, after we finally get out of bed and I coax her into the shower with me, which leads to some very hot fun. We get dressed and Zoey tries to teach me to cook, something which I thought would bore the pants off me, but with her there, guiding me, I liked it.

We eat pasta together, and everything feels so damn natural. Hand in glove is the expression. Everything fits.

She tells me how her dad left when she was young, her mom died of cancer at a too-young age, and her grandparents were there through it all. She wasn't a child when her mom died, she was in college, but the sadness is something that I didn't expect to affect me. The quiet dignity, and her acceptance. The way she shows it, but doesn't twist it into a crutch. It just all is.

Soft blues play in her little cozy living room. The furniture is lived in, old and unfashionable by any decorator's standard, but the plaid armchair and floral sofa and eclectic art on the walls suit her, and it creates that feeling of home. I can see the place was filled with love over the years.

And I'm almost disgusted with myself.

Zoey looks at me over the top of her hot chocolate. "You seem different."

"I do?" I keep my face and voice light and neutral.

She nods. "There have been little peeks here and there of other layers of you, but...last night was like I saw you."

"I needed a job, Zoey," I say, knowing I slipped up. I try and regret it, but I can't. "I was on my best behavior."

Leaning forward on the sofa, she smiles and takes a sip of the hot chocolate. "I think I like you more. As long as this is you."

A strange pang hits me, but I nod. "It is."

It's not until dark shadows start to stretch that it occurs I've been there all day, just hanging out with her. And I like it.

I don't know what the fuck that even means.

A message lights up my phone as I'm getting ready to leave. I have a fake gran to take care of, and actual business to do. With the time moving closer to having to prove I have heart, I have things to do. And I need to work on this.

The longer the Zoey thing goes, on, the longer she holds out, I mean, the more money I lose.

"I have to go."

"Your gran?"

"Yeah." My phone lights up again. I have someone I need to meet, so it's an easy enough lie. "I'll see you at work, Zoey."

I go to head down the stairs when she speaks. "This thing with you and me..." Her violet eyes are big as she looks at me.

"One day at a time, right?" I say.

"Right."

My dinner date turns into drinks. Michaela Emmerton is dressed for sex and seduction. It doesn't take any type of genius to work that out.

She's gorgeous, rich, and ruthless. My type.

So putting aside the night and day spent with Zoey, I can't quite work out why I'm not interested.

She's in town from the UK and I know her unspoken offer is, as always on the table. We've hooked up in the past and it's been hot. And now...

In this upscale bar on the Upper East Side, I'm interested in business but nothing else. Michaela leans in, tracing a long-nailed finger along a vein in my hand.

"Magnus?"

She's been talking to me, and I sip my tequila that's so smooth and smoky it might be mistaken as single malt by an untutored tongue, but the agave gives it that extra level. I stare into my heavy-based glass, then at her. "Distracted. Sorry."

"I was suggesting we take this meeting to my suite." She raises a brow. "Or not."

"Here is good for now. I've got a heavy week."

And she strokes a finger on my throat. "And someone on your mind?"

Fuck... I pull her hand away, and am about to get back onto the investment and donation at hand when something grabs my attention.

I glance up, and there, across the other side of the curved open bar is Suzanna.

Zoey's friend.

Something heavy slams like a lead wrecking ball into my stomach.

Shit...meet fan.

# Chapter Sixteen

## ZOEY

My fingers are numb and cold and a trickle of ice moves down my spine.

I look at Suzanna who is so out of place in the no frills bar with her hot red dress and heels. She bounces a foot and tosses her hair over her shoulder and the men in O'Reilly's devour every move.

Well, the ones who are straight and aren't accompanied by any kind of other half. Although they sneak looks, too.

I make myself lift my chin and I shrug. "I don't own him."

"It's not about ownership. You've kissed and…you should have seen that woman." She grabs her breasts pushing up her cleavage and above the music a glass smashes.

We've done way more than kiss. I can still feel Magnus touching me. Magnus inside me. And—I don't own him, like I said.

I'm sure if I say that enough it won't hurt.

He told me—more or less—he was seeing his grandmother.

But again…I don't own him.

"She makes me look flat chested." Suzanna stops, and has the grace to blush. "I mean…look, I worry about you, and I've seen how you look at him."

If I tell her he stayed last night, if I tell her what happened, she's liable to find some kind of weapon and go Villanelle on him.

"I don't look at him like anything."

She leans forward and nearly knocks over the Jack and Coke she insisted I have. "You kissed him. And it's me. You can't lie." Suzanna sighs. "I don't want you hurt."

"I don't even know what was happening."

"He was with some hot woman. What more do you want? I'll maim him."

"No. You won't."

"Look Bronn—"

"Was college. I've had other boyfriends—"

"Bronn was the big one."

I sigh. "I wasn't really in love with him. It was my ego. He betrayed me by cheating. That's his type. Rich and an asshole. And Magnus..."

Stopping, I pick up my drink and take a sip.

Magnus is complicated. He works for me, but we're not together. He's transient. That man isn't going to want to stay working in my store and I don't expect him to. And I refuse to entertain the thought I'm not going to have the store. Or the building.

My feelings are complicated.

The ice and cold in me is linked to Bronn, but it's the cheating. And I've been with guys, dated, had a boyfriend here and there, I'm not a nun, but...

To go from me to another woman is so skanky that I don't want him near me. If that's what happened.

I'm aware I'm floating above this, because what else is there to do? Fall apart? I don't love Magnus. I don't know him. Last night, today...that seemed to be him. It felt right, down deep in my bones. Not that he's not him, the other him, the one who's nice and pleasant. And I'm not saying that the man last night, the man today, wasn't a nice guy. I'm saying that man felt real. That man had meat and depth and substance behind nice.

But what if that's all an act and he's some kind of philanderer?

I can't ask.

Can I?

"Magnus works for me."

Suzanna laughs. "With added kissing and a sprinkling of the bookstore version of office romance." But she looks at me in total seriousness. "I want you happy, not hurt. So that's why I told you."

"Am I meant to ask?" I shake my head. "As I said, I don't know what was happening, and—"

"He saw me and you can act like a cucumber from the crisper all you want, but you don't fool me. You like him."

"Thanks, Suze," I say. "I'll deal with it tomorrow."

She pins me with a look as something raucous and drum beat heavy starts up on the loud speakers. "How? Do you need moral support?"

"I'll be fine."

And how? I guess I'll think of something.

"Anything you want to get off your chest?"

The next day, close to closing, Magnus finally comes down from the depths of upper hell where I sent him, sorting and pricing books.

These are the dusty ones that have been shoved up in the back of the storage room. I usually use those for sales, even though I know there are gems in there. I like that. The thrill of finding a table of books for sale for a couple of dollars and finding your version of the holy grail, or, you know, a gem, is fun. So those are the books I keep for those occasions.

I made him sort them, label the groups and put irrelevant prices on them.

Maybe, somewhere deep down, I am angry.

He told me he was seeing his gran. He must have seen Suzanna...although the woman he was with, Suze said she was hot. And for Suzanna to say that, the woman must have been smoking with a dash of extra ghost chili kinda hot.

But...even if his date was that level, Suze mentioned right off the bat he'd seen her. And he hadn't said a word.

All day long I've waited, but not one word.

Then again, what's he going to say, 'hey, had a great time banging your brains out, but funny story, I had to run off to see this super-hot woman.'

And now he's asking *me* if I've anything *I* want to say?

I squeeze my hands into fists, take a breath, and turn.

Magnus leans against the doorway where the stairs are, and the slow, low-lidded look he gives me makes my traitorous stomach flutter and things deep inside throb and sing with need.

He looks so good. That dark hair, those onyx eyes, the leanly muscled lines of him, those long legs in denim.

I might hate him.

I turn and stomp over to the counter. And I grab a cookie. They're free. Giving them away, all of them, eats into my budget a little, but considering I usually give away at least half, it's not a big deal. It's just the principle of it.

"Are you pissed off about that visit?"

"What do you mean?"

"I mean," he says, his hand closing over mine, "you're staring at the cookie like it's the worst criminal you've seen."

"Maybe it is." I take a vicious bite.

"Something is up. What is it?"

He's behind me now and he feels warm and strong and there, and it would be so easy to just give myself over to the sweet bliss I know he can make bloom within me. "You need to stop that."

For a moment I think he's going to argue or pretend he doesn't know what I'm talking about. But Magnus sighs and steps back, letting go of my hand.

And I'm not sure if I'm relieved or annoyed.

"Zoey." Magnus leans on the counter near me. "Do you really think I'm the kind of guy to go from one woman's bed right to another's?"

The cookie crumbles into chunks as my fingers squeeze down. "I don't know. Are you?"

Magnus straightens and rubs a hand over his face. "This thing with you and me—"

"There isn't a you and me."

"Then why are you so mad?"

"What makes you think I'm mad?" I sweep up the small pieces of cookie and dump them on the plate I used earlier.

"Everything."

I glare up at him and wish I hadn't. Because those dark eyes lock onto me and the tension and awareness in the air thickens and buzzes. My breath is caught hard in my lungs and the layers of him seem to treble. It's like Magnus is both being caring and trying to work me out in a way that borders on calculating.

Or else I am mad.

"I don't know what you're talking about."

"Don't you? I'm gonna assume you spoke to your friend."

I suck in a sharp breath. "Whatever you do outside of here isn't my business."

"Isn't it?"

That expression in his gaze morphs into something larger, deeper, and I look away. "You know it isn't. This is a bookstore. You're not staying."

"This isn't about the store, or the job."

"Look...that was yesterday, okay? A moment out of time. We...we fed a need in each other. It happens all the time."

Magnus laughs and squeezes my hand a moment. "Zoey, of all the things you can say, you choose something so not you?"

"But you don't know me." I frown at him.

He raises a brow. "I work with you—"

"For what? Two weeks?"

"And I've watched you. I've an interest."

"A passing one. I'm here." I snatch my hand away and step back, and he doesn't follow. No one is here in the store. It's close to closing and Mondays are always slow. And I'm more than aware I'm feeding into my own defense mechanisms, but what else can I do? Let someone who's transient in my life in beyond the physical? It's already gone further with him than it should.

People think I'm soft, and I am. But that doesn't mean I can't comprehend what's good for me and what isn't. And letting him touch me, getting to know me, getting to know him, that's...that's all good in its place. It's good as long as I don't attach meaning to it.

"And," I continue before he can speak, "you can do whatever you like."

He nods and a hardness comes to his gaze, almost like he's angry. "So your friend tells you, what? She saw me out last night? I'm assuming that's what happened because she's that type. Loyal."

"It's not my business."

"I didn't sleep with Michaela. Whom I met last night."

"We aren't dating."

Magnus frowns. "We had sex."

"So?"

He just stares at me, like he's going to say something, but instead he steps back, shaking his head and he pushes his hand through his hair. This time, when he looks at me, it's the placid, nice Magnus.

"I guess nothing. Maybe I read more into it than I thought. But I never said anything because..." He blows out a breath and leans against the counter, folding his arms. "Because I thought you'd ask. I've known her for a while. But every time I tried to think of how to bring it up, it just sounded like an excuse since your friend saw us...and now I'm making a mess of things."

The soft smile melts me a little.

"Magnus—"

The bell rings above the door and it opens. An old lady with a walker comes in and her eyes light up, even as she's short of breath. She has pin curls and gray-white hair, and she looks from Magnus to me.

"Gran. What are you doing?"

My heart lurches sideways. Magnus rushes to her side, but she swats him away with ineffectual moves and I'm turning into goo at the caring and fussing he shows. Call me a sucker, but there's something wonderful about a man who cares for his old grandmother. And it drives home what he's done for her, because I suspect the things he's told me have been so downplayed.

He might not be good at this job, but I'm betting he was fantastic at his chosen career, and...I'm letting my heart really get in the way.

"Stop your fussing, Magnus. I went out for a walk. I needed some air. And I thought...why not come see who the girl is you've been talking to me about? I'm Amanda, Magnus's gran. Do you want to come over for dinner?"

There was no way I could say no.

The little rundown apartment is only a couple of blocks away, and it makes me hate the Sinclair family more. Because that's who it's owned by. And Edward Sinclair, my nemesis, is the owner and is jacking up the rent.

His gran—Amanda—tells me this in a loud whisper as Magnus deals with dishes. She pats my hand as she sits on her recliner. I look around at the place. It's old and sparse and small.

She follows my gaze. "I can barely afford this place now. When my lease is up..." She sighs and shakes her head, giving my hand another pat.

"Your grandson's going to do whatever it takes to stop that. And I'll help, too." There's so much I want to say, there are things I wish I could do, but I can't save her home. I can't do anything.

"They wanted Magnus to move to London, did you know that? He tells me he wanted a change, so he left marketing, but I think he did that for me."

It hurts for some reason, that idea of Magnus no longer in New York. But he'll find something to fit his skills, and pay him more than I ever could. I don't know why he doesn't do that, anyway. And it's not like we're dating.

Then there's the sadness and guilt in her gaze and I smile. "I think your grandson does whatever he wants to do."

"I know. I just don't want him to throw his life away."

"I don't think he sees you like that."

"He won't leave me, no matter what I say." The old lady shakes her head. "It worries me."

"He'd hate you to worry." I smile as brightly as I can as I sit on the old sofa next to her. "There'll be other jobs for him. He's smart."

His gran chuckles and coughs, breathing hard. Magnus comes running. "Are you okay? Do you need anything?"

"No. Just like I told you when you came over last night. I'm fine." She says this sharply, like it's a conversation they've had a billion times, and it contains a warning tone. "Just worn out."

"We need to head out, anyway," he says. "C'mon, Gran. Go lie down."

The old lady nods. "You're a good boy. And I like her."

"Gran…" He slides an embarrassed look my way.

Amanda lets him help her up and lead her away. "I hope to see you again, Zoey," she says, "I like you…"

"I didn't expect her to turn up," Magnus says, walking me home.

It's a quiet Monday in this part of Bushwick, for the neighborhood. There are a lot of apartment buildings perched on top of shops, and buildings with stoops that lead directly to the street.

We're a block away from my store and home, but I stop. He stops, too. I look up at him in the streetlamps. "She's lovely."

I don't know what it is I want to say, only there's something there, pressing at me, and he's watching, like he's waiting to follow my lead.

"Yeah."

"And she cares about you."

"Zoey, thanks for coming."

He touches my cheek and I almost sigh in the cool night air. "Of course."

"Even though you're mad at me." Magnus smiles, flashing the dimple.

"I'm not...I..." I breathe out. "I...I don't know why you don't find something suited where you can make more money."

He sighs. "It's a rock and a hard place."

"What is?"

He takes my hand and kisses it, and instead of making me swoon, it makes me frown. I like him. Okay, I can admit that, but I can't let a man addle my brain.

"Work, looking after Gran, making ends meet at least until I can work things out."

I nod. I'm halfway to letting myself accept this because it's not my business, not really, when all of a sudden, I can't stop myself.

"There are pieces of you, Magnus, that I can't make fit, no matter how often I turn them."

"People are complicated."

I nod slowly. "Yeah, but you... Who is she to you?"

"Gran?" That smile again. "Or who I had to meet after I saw gran last night?"

My stomach knots. "Don't play games with me," I say quietly. "I can't stand it and I don't deserve it. So who is she and why were you at one of the most exclusive places in Manhattan?"

# Chapter Seventeen

## MAGNUS

For someone full of sweetness and light, with marshmallows tumbling in her veins, Zoey is way tougher than she looks.

I'm not a fucking idiot. I know exactly what she's asking.

Amelia, who apparently decided to call herself Amanda, did well. Turning up at the right moment. But I need to sort this out first.

The stupid part is, nothing happened with Michaela. It was business. It could have turned into something more, but I chose not to, and Michaela was fine with that either way.

Zoey's bombshell of a friend who has money and clearly dates very moneyed men is a wrench in the works, but one I'm about to use and spin into gold.

Not the friend, per se, but the fact I was with Michaela at Jones' Bar.

I squash the little bursts of guilt that flare. After all, I need Zoey's place. I need to get my plans moving on the heart front, or moving further than where they are. And Michaela is a good way to do it.

But now I need to slightly spin things to fit.

"For someone who doesn't care, you seem to care, Zoey." I lean in and whisper my next words against her ear, and breathe in her scent. "I like it."

"Magnus..."

I straighten up. "I told you how I was ready to move and I lost my job..."

I take a deep breath, like I'm telling her a dark secret, and the ping of unease in my bones helps. Of course it does, I'm creating a mood. I like her, she's just caught in my plans and she'll be compensated more than fairly, so I'm not feeling anything like guilt. Magnus Simpson does, over his dear gran, and that's all it is.

"Thing is, Zoey, I never told you why. I needed to move on to help my grandmother. If I stayed in marketing, took another job, it would be long hours, way too many hours..."

"I don't know much about the corporate world," she says as I pause. I've paused to give myself space to think of the next words, and to gague her response. "But...I imagine it's just like that."

"You're not going to suggest I should have hired someone to look after her?"

"No! She's got her faculties. She's strong. She reminds me a little of Tuesday Harry. Of my own grandma. They're old, not imbeciles. People treat old people terribly. But not you. I think...I think you're a good man. And you're doing the right thing. I admire you."

Okay, that might be a little guilt I feel, but I squash it dead. It's just from hanging out with Zoey all day. She's dangerous to black hearts everywhere. And she's useful to me in a lot of ways.

"I worked with her, Michaela. She took me for drinks to try and talk me into working in the UK. I said no. That's all. I also tried to get her to donate to that charity, where we went."

She looks at me, her big eyes soft and sweet and she rises on her toes and kisses me and it takes everything I am not to grab her here and now. "You're a good man, Magnus Simpson."

"Come on." I take her hand. "I'll walk you to your door."

As her fingers close around mine, I don't probe why I'm not pushing this.

Getting this over and done with means I can concentrate on the heart of the job, and using Zoey is something that could work, but I don't let that linger, not right now. Because she's a little too good at reading me—perhaps not what goes on behind the Magnus Simpson mask, but the fact something's going on, and that doesn't help.

Back at the bookstore, I follow her inside and help her pack up the few cookies left over and the slices of cake. She doesn't ask, I merely help. We work together in quiet companionship, and finally, when everything's done, I take hold of her face in my hands and lift it to mine.

"Zoey, you helping me makes a world of difference. I might not seem that way, but it does. Gran's...frail, and I had to turn down the job offer, just like I did last night. I..."

I brush her lips with mine and they're so soft and warm and tremble a little beneath my mouth. That shiver of need from her, a need that's loaded in ways I don't want to fathom, shoots to my cock, yes, but it also shoots through my blood, heating me inside.

"It's okay," she says, her hands covering mine a moment, those big violet eyes pools I could lose myself in—Magnus Simpson could lose himself in—search mine, "I get it. She doesn't want to leave, and I'm sorry I asked you about your friend and why you went to that bar—"

"Hey..." I smile at her. "I'd ask to, roles reversed."

I want to kiss her. It's a beat of need in my blood, the yearn for the pleasure she contains, the real heat of her that can coil about me, become the sweetest invasion, but I don't. Just brush her mouth with mine, lingering once again.

"I'll see you tomorrow, Zoey."

"Goodnight."

I wait for her to lock the door behind me, and then I set off in the direction Magnus Simpson lives. It's not until I've turned the corner I call my car service to collect me.

As I settle in the leather seat of the town car, I close my eyes as we head back to Manhattan and my office. It's early enough—for me, and I tell myself I left without kissing her because it's part of my plan.

Make her really want more of Magnus Simpson.

But a tiny voice that won't shut up keeps asking if Magnus Sinclair is running away.

Because like it or not, Zoey affects me, too.

"Why are you here?" I scowl at Ryder as he breezes into my home.

"I was in your hood."

"You never come here unless you want something." I pour a drink and throw myself on the black leather sofa in my living room. Ryder picks up the tequila bottle, sniffs it, shrugs, and does the same, adding a big splash of soda water to his.

He sits on the sofa opposite and turns the glass in his hands. "Just wondering how things are going?"

"I'm working on the girl."

Ryder frowns. "The bookstore thorn in your side girl?"

"Yeah, I—"

I stop abruptly as heat prickles my skin.

"I was talking about the Sinclair jewels. You remember those, right, Mag? The Sinclair flagship? Our father's weird-ass plan from the great beyond?" Ryder looks at me, like he's studying a bug. "You like her."

"She's easy to like, if you like that sort of thing," I say smoothly. "Zoey's sweet. But stubborn."

"You're more sex and steel than sweet and stubborn. And..." He points at me with his glass, "you slept with her."

My fingers tighten on my drink. "Why would you say that?"

"You did, didn't you?"

"When did you turn into Mr. Morals? It happened. So what?"

Ryder rests his glass on his thigh and draws shapes on the arm of his sofa with a finger. "Oh, nothing. Just you know, big, bad, Mr. Power and Money Sinclair slept with someone sweet. Notice how I didn't say fuck? I used that old euphemism, slept. Because I saw you at that dumb party with her, and—"

"Do you have a point?" I glare at my brother. "If you're concerned about this interfering with the rat maze I'm being made to run through, don't be. I'm able to multitask."

He sighs. "You can do that. I'm aware. But I'm also aware you usually crush someone like this woman to get what you want."

"Crush is harsh." It's true, but I follow the line of the law. I'll skate close to the edge, but it's more pleasing to see how I can push rules. And... I frown. "If I crush her, then all my good work is moot here."

"So, you don't need to move yet on your project."

"If you want the damn earrings, you can have them."

Ryder gives me a contemplative look. "I'm not sure it works that way. They're marked for you."

"I don't have anything to wear with them. Besides, my ears aren't pierced."

He takes a long swallow of his tequila. "You're funny, dickwad, really."

"Hey, you're the one who's mostly obsessed with them."

"Yeah." He stares into his glass for a long moment. "But you notice how things shifted after Hud got his ring? We've all discussed this, but our father's up to something."

"He's dead."

"That's not going to ever stop him making a point." Ryder laughs softly. "And you know what I mean. There's something bigger and the fact these up until recently only rumored about family heirlooms are turning up, tied into the Sinclair flagship, I don't know…I don't want any of us to fuck this up."

"By that, you mean me."

He sets the glass down and stands, hands in the pockets of his jeans as he goes to the window and leans against the frame, looking out into the dark. "I think you're doing something morally…not okay."

"Not okay?" I take a swallow of my drink. It should warm me, not send a shiver of ice through my blood. "As in reprehensible?"

"I think you doing this might negate whatever good you're going to do to show you have heart." He breathes out. "Whatever the fuck that means."

He's got that right. "So I let this be until after all of this?"

"It's only two weeks."

"Our mother met her."

"I know." Ryder turns and looks at me. "What are you going to do?"

It's a good question, and I do have answers. I'm going to take Zoey's place. But perhaps I can hold off, no matter how I go from wanting to eke it out to rushing it so I'm not stained by her goodness. That shit eats down deep.

"I have a foundation ready to go. I have charities. I'm giving all over the place. Some of them I'm not even going to use for taxation purposes."

Ryder rolls his eyes. "That's what accountants and business managers are for. The bottom dollar matters, I know that, but don't screw up and lose our heritage."

Now I stand, too, and go and pour myself another tequila, straight. "I'm not about to. The Sinclair name, our family company, they mean something, and they add something to all of our brands. They give us depth. I'm not about to let a little curly haired creature get in my way."

My brother just gives me a look that says the world. And I get it, I do. Zoey has a way of getting in the way, of sliding down deep, of causing the kind of trouble I never expected.

Zoey can be a backburner project for the next two weeks. I can manipulate things to my advantage, go in less until this other situation is dealt with, and then finish with a perfect landing.

Actually, knowing my mother, I wouldn't put it past her to keep an eye on the Zoey thing, even talk to Jenson. But I can manipulate that, too. Set up something to take care of Zoey. Make it look like my plan was that all the time.

And the more I think, the more I start to reshape my plan, and my fake gran sits in the center, with Zoey, with the Sinclair jewels, with my father's meddlesome ways for me to keep the balance of our heritage in the proper hands—those belonging to me and my brothers. I can use it all to show I have heart.

I smile at Ryder. "Don't worry. I have a plan."

It's almost midnight when my phone rings. I think of ignoring it as I'm neck deep in work, setting things up. But it's Georgio. I hit answer on my phone and his voice fills the room.

"We got a problem, Boss."

"This problem got a name?"

"Bronn Lichtenfeld."

Fuck.

# Chapter Eighteen

## Zoey

The insistent buzzing of my cell drags me rudely into wakefulness. I grab it from the coffee table and burrow down beneath the throw. "Hello?"

"Babe, it's me."

It takes me an embarrassingly long time to place the voice. "Who?" I sit up slowly and push my hair from my face. "Bronn?"

"We should catch up."

"After how many years?" I couldn't sleep last night and ended up baking until four a.m. So I'm not in the mood.

For a moment he doesn't answer, and then he says, "Is the flame still burning for old Bronn?"

Good God, talk about inexplicable choices. "No flame," I say to him. "Just tired, and you're the last person I expected to hear from. And I don't have time to—"

"We'll cut to the chase. I hear Sinclair's sniffing around and you haven't sold. I want to make an offer..."

Where Bronn made me annoyed, Magnus makes me melt. I know I should have pushed to see if my college ex had any dirt on Edward Sinclair, but what am I going to do with it? Pot plants?

Even if these high-powered bullies all play nasty games, and play them sloppily, that's not me.

I don't have a chance down in the muck, even if I wanted to, and the muck isn't okay. Sinking to other people's low bars is wrong. And…I'm not playing games.

Besides, a guy like Bronn isn't going to give me anything. That's not out of intelligence, although I know he isn't stupid. It's out of his greed and his self-satisfaction with being born into the right family. I imagine Edward Sinclair is exactly the same. They just both want.

They're shallow, egotistical assholes. They think about their ambitions, making money, power, and Magnus… He gave up his career—or put it on hold—for his gran. He lost his job because to take the promotion, to work in the arena he's trained in, he knew he wouldn't have the room to do what he considers right.

He's layered and complex and a man who, I think, can see past the almighty dollar.

Because why else would he be here? In my store?

The ease, yes, the freedom, definitely, but there are other jobs to make him money. He chose having the time to flex so he could spend it with his gran, to keep an eye on her. That's depth.

And me? I'm exactly where I was, still trying to keep my home and business from falling into callous, moneyed hands.

The bell dings and the man who makes me melt walks in. There's no one else here as I've just opened, but his smile when his eyes meet mine makes my heart sing all kinds of songs that it shouldn't.

After Bronn's call, it hit me that I haven't had a visit from anyone to do with Sinclair since the whole power outage and the street work. I'd love to say they must have changed their minds, but I know they haven't. Life doesn't work that way and I'm waiting.

"You look both tired and preoccupied."

I shake my head. "That's no way to talk to women." I duck behind the counter and give him a cookie I know he's not going to eat. It's cranberry, white chocolate, and dark sugared pecans today. Then I set about making coffee.

"Beautiful is a given."

I slide him a look, even as warmth spreads through me. It might be a terrible line said as a joke but I'll take it. "Don't push it."

He comes up and leans over the counter as I set his espresso down. Magnus shifts it out of the way and takes my hands, his onyx eyes crinkling in the corners as he smiles. "You are, you know. Beautiful. Inside and out."

He sucks in a breath and straightens, letting me go and fussing with his caffeine fix. His words make me reel and I stir in sugar after sugar into mine.

"I'm okay. Just couldn't sleep and then..." I sigh. "My ex called this morning."

Magnus goes still. "Oh?"

"Yeah. I guess he heard I hadn't sold and wanted to make me an offer. I'm guessing so he could then use his money to get more from Sinclair."

"Or a piece of the project," he mutters. He casts me a long look. "Did you take it up?"

"Have you met me?" I take a sip of my coffee and almost choke. It's caffeinated sugar with a little milk. I set it down.

Magnus takes my hand before I can move away. "I think I do. You're not going to sell to him, or to Sinclair, no matter what."

I just smile and shake my head. "I'm that obvious?"

"I think you're that principled."

Words bubble up, and his hand is warm and solid and reassuring on mine and I want to tell him how lovely he is, but I'm saved from making a fool of myself by the bell.

Mikey comes in and his eyes dart between me and Magnus and his hand on mine. I go to pull away but Magnus's fingers tighten a little and then he lets me go.

"Is he bugging you, Mama S?"

Magnus's gaze hits mine, full of heat and humor and something much darker, like a proprietary spark that sends a deep thrill tumbling in my blood. "Am I, Mama S?"

There's something in his tone that's made of steel, that's like a sliver of danger and that thrill dissipates. Mikey, for all his bluster, is insecure, and he's the exact right age where being made fun of, mocked by a man like Magnus, might cause wounds.

"No one's bothering me, Mikey," I say.

"There you go." Magnus straightens up, and turns his cup on the counter. "You're a good man, Mikey."

Mikey's eyes narrow and his body tenses like he's waiting for the blow. "I like her. She's good people."

"I know." Magnus leans into the kid a little. "And she's naïve as all hell. She needs someone savvy to keep his eye out. Glad to know you're on the job."

Mikey searches his face a long time like he's looking for the hidden meanings, but then he relaxes, nods, puffs up a bit, and straightens his cap.

"Always," the kid says.

And I relax, too. Magnus excuses himself, grabs the duster and goes to the books, straightening them, dusting as he goes and Mikey shakes his head.

I fill up a bag with cookies and a couple of slices of cake. I made a nut and seed cake today. It's healthy, but tastes good. Perfect for Mikey. I hand them to him with a couple of books I set aside I think he'll like.

"Your boyfriend—"

"He works here."

Mikey rolls his eyes. "He's not bad people, Mama S. Catch ya on the flip side."

He leaves and I pick up the crumpled fiver the kid left on the counter and put it in the register, marking a little card I keep for Mikey under the register drawer.

My hand shakes as awareness burns into me and I look up into Magnus's gaze. His mouth twists, then he says, "I'll be back in a few."

I can't help it. I follow him to the door and watch as he darts across the traffic to catch Mikey.

Magnus does most of the talking, but Mikey finally nods, and they pull out their phones, like they're swapping numbers. The moment Magnus turns, I hurry back to the counter and start sorting the piles of things I need to do tonight. Like bookkeeping. The bell dings and he just smiles at me as he approaches.

"Not going to ask?"

"Ask what?"

"Why I chased after Mikey?"

I shrug and he leans over the counter, brushing against my hand and making me shiver as he grabs the card and holds it up. I snatch it away and slide it back.

"You have an account for him, don't you?"

Heat floods my skin. "It's not much. Just when he gives me money, I record it and put away for him. That's all."

"You're like a saint without all the annoying parts."

"Are saints annoying?" I pick up the books and paperwork and hug them.

"I'm pretty sure sanctimonious counts as annoying."

"Why did you go after him?"

He rubs a hand over the back of his neck. "Not to be sanctimonious. I just figured I could help him out."

Magnus glances away a moment.

"It's just some after school stuff, to do with the charity we went to. And I know how you feel about Sinclair, but…"

I come around the counter and give him a one-armed hug, breathing in his whiskey, dark citrusy scent, letting myself indulge in the heat of him for a moment. "That's sweet."

"I'm not sweet."

I draw back. "You are, you know. Magnus-style sweet. And…I think you're ready."

"Don't look at me like I'm a baby bird."

"I'm not throwing you from a nest. I'm just going to duck into the back for a big part of the day, leave you to it. I have bookkeeping and other boring mundane things to do."

Magnus doesn't move and while I'm not expecting fireworks and leaps for joy, I don't expect this. I don't expect the stillness and the strange look on his face, but then he smiles. "Okay. I promise I won't burn the place down."

And with that, I go to tackle all the things I don't want to, things I normally do in the evening. And for once, a touch of lightness comes over me. Maybe things are going my way.

Things going my way might be a little bit of a stretch, I decide hours later, but I'll take the tiny nuggets.

I worked through lunch, just grabbing a cookie and a coffee. And I'm not checking up on him, but he's with a customer, someone well-heeled, probably in from a few blocks over where the gentrification has set in. But she has books in her arms and Magnus is leading her towards the art books.

Smiling, I dive back into my little area and I smile deeper as the ding of the register sounds.

The day wears on and the normal sales happen and I let Magnus handle things because there are issues I have to deal with. Bills, and all the things that come with a business. There's an estate sale coming up and the area at the foot of the Catskills is full of little stores and pop up garage sales this time of year, and I want to go because I can usually find books. We do get people coming in with bags of books to sell to us, but these things always hold gems. And it's a nice way of collecting all sorts of books I might not normally be able to.

But getting all the grindstone work out of the way frees me up for such day trips.

Later in the afternoon, I join Magnus and the day passes into evening in a harmonious companionship.

One that's layered by an unspoken awareness and tension that drips with sexual innuendo.

Magnus finally flips the sign at the end of the day and sighs, leaning against the door. "Want me to close the register?"

"If you're ready."

He raises a brow. "I think I can handle it."

When that's done he's ready to leave, lingering and I'm doing the same. He approaches me slowly, and brushes a curl from my face, his fingers warm and gentle and a lick of flame rises in my belly.

"We're done for the day," he says.

"Yes."

"So since we're off the clock and you're not in boss mode, I can finally do what's been on my mind all day long."

Before I can even ask, he lowers his mouth to mine, kissing me soft and sweet, and the flame flares bright in me as I cling to him, kissing him back, letting the heat and magic melt into my bones.

He's like tinder to that flame in me. Tinder spiked with fuel. And the kiss morphs from sweet to erotic in seconds and a fierce hunger sweeps me. His arms are around me and he walks me back until I hit the counter. Then he lifts me like I don't weigh anything, and puts me there, on the top, and we're face to face.

The kisses come in slow and biting as he parts my jean-clad thighs and steps between them, moving against me, letting me feel the heat and steel of his erection and I moan into him, wrapping my arms about his neck, fingers thrust into his thick, soft hair as I tug his face to me and he takes my mouth deep.

Magnus moves a trail of fire over my chin and down my throat, his teeth nipping against my pulse point and he slides a hand up against my pussy, rubbing me slowly or am I rubbing against him. All that material is in the way and I want...I need...

Shit.

I break the kiss, gasping for air. "Magnus, the lights are on and the whole store front is glass."

"So?"

"I'm not into giving a show. And we—"

"Yeah, I know. Take it slow." He straightens and kisses the tip of my nose, his hands coming to rest on my thighs as he breathes in slow and steady. "Lucky for you, my phone started to buzz. I need to go." He pulls it out and the name Gran is on the screen. He shakes his head and sets it on the counter. "In a minute. I don't think anyone needs to see me like this."

I put my hands on either side of his face and bring it to mine. "You're a good man, Magnus Simpson."

The next morning, I'm alone in the store. I'm buzzing a little from last night. The sweetness of him before he left me, that underlying layer that draws me down into him.

And I'm glad I'm alone to breathe and think. There's an aura about Magnus that is overwhelming. To me.

He makes me want to lose myself.

So when he texted to say he'd be in at lunch, I was happy. Well, happy isn't exactly the right word. He said it wasn't anything to worry about, just he needed to make some last-minute appointments.

The doorbell dings and I turn. Magnus's gran, Amanda, shuffles in, seemingly frailer than she was last time I saw her.

I hurry to help her. "Magnus isn't here."

"Oh. That boy…He's probably doing what I asked him not to. Meeting my doctors."

"Are you okay?"

She pats my hand. "It's just a small operation, dear. Nothing to worry about."

And then to my horror, her face crumples.

"That, I can put off. You can't tell him about this. Promise."

"Whatever it is, tell him."

"No. He's given up so much. I…can't."

My stomach knots. "Amanda, what happened?"

"It's that beast who bought my building. He's putting up all the prices. If I can't pay, and pay the back rent, I'm out. And I've nowhere to go."

# Chapter Nineteen

## MAGNUS

It's been a hell of a morning. I've been at it since five a.m.

It's ten now, and I need to head to Zoey's store soon.

Thing is, my leisurely timeline to do with her store is now fast track. Tapping my pen against the leatherbound notebook on my desk in my office, I glare at my notes. I should have known the longer it took me to close all the deals and crush the last holdout—Zoey—into dust that the hyenas and vultures would come sniffing.

Bronn Lichtenfeld won't mention me by name, so that's not a worry. I don't like him and I've met him a few times, but I don't have to know someone not to like them. I learn a lot by watching how people conduct business and he's about money. Shallow, vulgar in that Lichtenfeld way.

He, or I'm betting his father, has seen what I'm buying up and knows it's big. They're in banking but they like to invest in money makers no matter what. If it's got the name Sinclair attached, then...

No. He's not going to mention Magnus to Zoey, although his calling her sent a jolt through me yesterday. He's going to try and buy her out. She won't do it. But his sniffing about, or rather his sniffing about properties in the area, means I have to push fast forward.

I've no intention of giving him money, of paying overblown prices to an overblown ego. And I've also no intentions of sharing anything I'm doing. Especially this project.

What I need to do is up the gran game, which I've set in motion. Part Zoey with money for dear old gran.

It's not like I'm going to let her sink, at least not now. She'll get it all back and I'll save her, making everything come together.

But I need to get at her books. As in the ones with the numbers. And I've got a special charity ready to launch, one of the reasons I spoke to the kid.

I was more than aware of one wrong move with him and the kid would take it the wrong way. Worse, Zoey would have as well, and I don't want to disappoint her.

As part of the game, of course.

I rub my hand against my chest, like I can dislodge the sudden cold lump that feels a little like regret and foreboding, but is probably hunger.

If I get the kid on board, get him some work, it gives him purpose, and it makes me look good in Zoey's eyes. And down the track, when she comes crashing down along with her store, well, she'll remember that.

"You look like you're both plotting and the world is weighing you down."

I flick my glance up at my mother. "I'm getting a new personal assistant."

"Please. I'm your mother. An employee can't stop me."

"You have other children. Don't you want to terrorize one of them?"

My mother pulls out a chair and elegantly sits down, smoothing her hands along the front of her tailored skirt. "They're not the ones who are trying to keep hold of the Sinclair jewels and the company, Magnus."

I pick up a matte black folder from my desk and toss it to her. She catches it with a grimace and opens it, flipping through the thick hand cut paper inside.

She closes it and sets it down. "Impressive."

"Heart, mother. That's a whole lot of heart there. Think Jenson and his little team will be impressed?"

"No doubt."

I narrow my eyes at her.

"But thing is, I'm going to be judging you."

"So it's all good."

"I told you this is more complicated than you might be thinking, Magnus. Heart isn't just money."

"Money helps and you know it."

"Money, Magnus, isn't the only way."

I spread my hands. "You told me three-legged puppies were out. I'm actually doing good things."

"You are, and I commend you."

"Well?"

She sighs and leans forward, hand on my desk. "Well, what?"

"You were there at one of my charity events. And that—" I point my pen at the folder "—is a billion-dollar foundation I'm setting up. Does my dead father want blood?"

She stands suddenly, her face a cool mask. "Don't, Magnus. That level of callous disregard is—"

"What he made me and you know it. And I'm not complaining. I'm fantastic at what I do, Mother. I care about the legacy of our family company, but between you and me, I don't give a shit about earrings. If it was just the company, I'd probably let all these stupid games he's making me play go. But my brothers care. So... here I am. A performing monkey."

"That isn't what this is about, Magnus." She crosses to the floor to ceiling window and stares a moment out into the gunmetal gray day.

I follow her. "Then tell me. I'll save the damn jewels so Ryder can get his share, and the company to keep everyone happy. And I'll do it without wasting time."

She looks up at me. "Your father had some kind of plan he wants played out. He wasn't a good husband..."

He wasn't a good father, either, but I keep that to myself. Because it's not really something I've focused on in the way I am now. And my mother...we're closer to her than we were to him. But he had a variety of wives, all younger versions of my mother. And so I don't get why or how she remained close to him. Love? Their fucked up version?

It's not my place and it's not my arena of life. Making money is.

"But he did love all of you."

I just nod. "Is that all?"

"How's the girl?"

"What girl?"

But she isn't buying it. My mother smiles. "Zoey."

Heat prickles down along my spine. "You remember her name?"

My mother places her palm against my shaved cheek. "I told you she's different from your usual type. And yes, I get you said you're helping her, but you looked at her in a way that I've never seen."

"Oh good God, please don't go reading into things."

I say this with sarcasm and intended bored cynicism. Except...except it doesn't come out that way. The words are soft, with a tinge of something I don't like, so I ignore them and she doesn't say a word.

She just looks past me to my desk. "You didn't open your present."

"I never got around to it. I've been busy. I can do it now."

"That wasn't my point..." My mother stops and shakes her head, sighing. "It's nothing much, Magnus, but it's not..." She shakes her head again. "Sometimes things are more than what they might seem."

"Like my foundation."

"Everything you've done looks good. Great even. But Magnus, I think it's worth repeating myself. Heart might not mean what you think it does. Money really isn't everything."

I laugh and cross the floorboards, back to my desk, my gaze falling on the neatly wrapped gift. She has a point, I should have opened it. That's the polite thing to do. But we don't give out that many gifts, not unless it's something coveted by one of us. After all, we can just buy shit ourselves.

And I'm not an idiot. I get the whole thought that counts bullshit.

"Money is, Mother, and you know it."

"Do I?"

I look at her, sitting on the corner of my desk as I pick up the small, light gift. "Yes. After all, why stay so close to our father? You're not the sadist type."

She just smiles and comes over and kisses my cheek. "I'll see you soon."

Faye Sinclair walks out of my office and I can't shake the feeling her whole visit held something more than I'm getting. With a sigh, I check my watch. I need to check in with Gran. I need to get to Zoey's books soon. And then, I need to bring the next step into play.

I'm about to put the gift down when something stops me.

Guilt?

Curiosity?

I pull the paper off and dump it onto the desktop.

It's a long, flat, light black leather box. I open it, and inside, is a key.

The key's big, old fashioned, gold, with an intricate pattern engraved over it. The thing is beautiful, if you're into that kind of thing, but what the living fuck does it mean?

A bauble? Something to put on display? Who knows. I put it back in its box and close the lid, setting it down on the desk.

I don't have time for my mother's convoluted gift. I'll send her flowers and a thank you. I call through to my assistant and set that up.

Then, I grab my light coat to head out to the car I've got waiting.

I like details, so we head to Bushwick, to where I told Zoey Magnus Simpson has his apartment.

Once I'm inside, I grab a shower, and change into his clothes, jeans, T-shirt, sneakers, hoodie. The place is a studio and there isn't much here. But that fits. I don't intend to bring Zoey or anyone else here, but I've crashed a night or two, and if anything changes, if she wants to stop by, I have a place.

And then I'm ready to head out.

Inside my stomach is heavy and again, it's got to be hunger. After all, there's nothing to feel guilty about.

But there's a part of me that can't shake the feeling that if I was Magnus Simpson, I could bring her here. And there's a part of me that wishes things were different.

They're not.

And Zoey is a victim of circumstance, her place being in the wrong place for her. I know I wasn't going to give a damn, but it's hard not to. She's so likable. Moreish. I'll take care of her whether she wants it or not. And she'll be better off without that eyesore. Without her having to scrounge her way through life.

My phone buzzes as I'm locking up.

"Amelia?"

"Hello, dear," my fake gran says, "phase two is under way."

It's time to move.

# Chapter Twenty

## ZOEY

The changes in the neighborhood are fast, even if they've been a long time coming. It's Thursday and my mind is just overflowing with things. The rain that's been threatening pours down in the late afternoon. It's a slow day, with a few extra sales from people darting in to avoid the worst of the rain.

"Things change, Zoey," Magnus says behind me as I look out the window from the little front display I'm meant to be redoing.

"I know. But it shouldn't be because of a bully who wants to price people out." The last of the boxes go into the moving truck double parked outside. The warning lights are a beacon that breaks the gray. "That's the Abidi family moving out."

His fingers slide slow along the zipper of my dress and I shiver from that light touch. "Perhaps on to better pastures."

"Or further out, where commuting is a little more difficult for them."

"It's part of life."

I stiffen a little at the barely-there words, but he softens them.

"Or so they say. C'mon, Zoey, the day's pretty much done. You can't change things." He pushes my hair away from my neck, leaving it exposed to the warmth of his breath, and in the reflection I can see us, wavery with the rain outside, ghostly figures, and he leans down, almost skimming my skin with his lips.

"I want to."

I want to sink into him and just let him take me from all the worries, all the pressures that eat at me. I want to forget anything and everything and just feel.

"Maybe," he murmurs, his lips brushing my skin, "you have. Just by not giving in you've made them more money."

I turn and he's there, body skimming mine. "They rented. They got priced out by the landlord. And that happened because their no-good landlord sold to Sinclair to make a pretty penny."

With a small sigh he steps away from me and I turn back to my display, placing books and little boxes I found in the little room where odds and ends always find their way, right at the top of the stairs before roof access.

It's fall and boxes and old crates and lock boxes all make that feeling of hidden corners where you can unlock the secrets of books. That's the thought in my mind, anyway. And overall, I think it looks okay.

I dust my hands and try to find that sweet warmth that held promised passion from his touch, but the truck is still there. And now Sinclair's in my mind. Sinclair and the things Magnus doesn't know about his gran's situation.

She told me how he thinks she's paid up, but bills add up and she doesn't want him to foot them. How he's paying for elective surgery for her hip. Everything is a mess and if I had a million dollars I'd give it to those who need it.

But I don't.

A customer comes in and I let Magnus handle it, stepping into the back and going over some numbers I've been crunching for a couple of days. When the register door closes and the bell on the front door tinkles, I close the notepad with my sums and I step out behind the register.

We're both there, close enough to touch, close enough to feel the other's body heat. But I don't touch him, and he doesn't touch me. That little moment at the front of the store was only that; a moment. I pull up a stool and sit, then look up at Magnus.

"How's your gran?"

He shrugs. "Old. But stubborn."

"The mobility issues?" I half smile and reach for a ginger and cacao nib cookie I made. "I'm prying, I know. But...I liked her."

"She likes you."

"I just didn't expect the walker and her frailty. Not her spirit. That's strong, but bodies..."

"They give out, yeah, I know." He breathes out and closes his eyes for a moment. "It's one of the reasons I'm here. She needs an operation."

I might not have a million dollars, but I'm better off than most. Especially most around here, and I own this place; Sinclair and his evil goons notwithstanding. "I can help—"

"Zoey."

"What? I can. If it's pride, you need to swallow it down." I put my cookie down and cross my arms. "I don't say things I don't mean."

He stares at me a long time, those onyx eyes darkening and his expression—I can't read it, but it's not what I expect—bites down into me.

I expected him to land somewhere on my spectrum between embarrassment and grateful.

What I have is...not triumph, but I thought that flickered, although I put that down to the way his eyes catch the light...but something darker, graver, almost wonder but with a fatalistic edge. As I say, I can't read it.

Maybe it's shock.

"I know you don't. And it's stupid, Zoey. Stupid to wear your heart on your sleeve. People will take advantage."

"Then that's bad karma for them."

He runs his fingers lightly along my arm. "Probably. And thank you. I honestly don't know if you realize how much that means to me for you to say that. But we don't really know each other—"

"You help people. Otherwise, what have you got? A pile of emptiness? And as I said, you help people. People need to help other people, so—"

"No."

I frown and slowly get up from the stool. "No? But if you need help, then I can. I'm not asking for you to pay me back."

"I would, if I took your offer, but I'm not going to."

"And then I'd give you as long as you needed to do so. My offer's on the table."

"You don't even know how much it is."

"I'd give what I could."

"And I appreciate that, I do, but I can't take from you, Zoey."

I nod. Because now the idea is in my head. He's being some kind of prideful. "We could do a fundraiser—"

Magnus laughs. "Giving and helping that charity is enough to make my gran annoyed if she found out. Imagine if word got back, I'd started a fundraiser?"

"I think she'd secretly be happy."

"Zoey, leave it. I'll find a way."

When the mail comes, hand delivered by USPS, I can't get the urge to help out of my system.

I know things he doesn't.

And I made a promise not to say a word.

That promise doesn't stop me from trying to do something, though.

"Can you man the store for me for a while? If it hits six and I'm not back, just lock up and—"

"Leave the key under the mat? I'll wait for you to get back." He looks at me like he's expecting some kind of explanation, which makes sense. But he's not getting one.

I go into the back and grab my raincoat, umbrella, and bag. "I've got some errands to run. See you soon."

"Zoey! Come in."

I follow Amanda...actually, I'm not sure if she's Magnus's maternal or paternal grandparent...into her apartment.

"I'm so sorry, I didn't expect someone to come knocking."

"There's no security in this building."

She nods, picking up a knickknack from the mantle in one hand, the other clinging to the walker. His gran looks a little frailer, more drawn, but after what she told me, I don't blame her. And add that to what Magnus said...

"I know," his gran says, putting the knickknack down and she offers me a brave kind of smile. "The buzzer was broken ages ago, along with the lock. And this new landlord isn't going to fix anything."

"I'm not surprised. This is how the rich make their money, preying on others."

She nods again. "But what can we do?"

"Maybe you should talk to Magnus."

"No, he does enough for me. He-he's sunk so much of his savings and money and time into helping me out. He doesn't think I know all that, but I do. I can't ask him to pay my rent, too."

"I can help—"

"No dear. The prices are skyrocketing and I'm half convinced this place will be pulled down. It's happening all over." She eases down onto the armchair and sighs. "I'll be okay. I'll find a way."

"I can help."

"No, Zoey."

I nod. I can't force people to accept my help. But there has to be a way, help find a place nearby. Or…I don't know, I'll need to think of something.

"It doesn't have to be money."

"Oh, my grandson should never let you go. You're a keeper."

And heat floods me. That isn't what this is about. "At least think on it," I say, sidestepping the whole comment.

"I won't change my mind."

"Thinking on things can help," I say. I check my phone. I still need to visit the bank. "I need to go, but just think on it."

"Fine. I'll think on it." I'm almost at the door when she says, "Zoey, just one more thing…"

Nerves nip at me as I hurry back through the rain from the bank. I have a meeting set up and the more I let my idea stew in my head, the more I'm convinced I can do this. It's risky, but it's my decision.

I go into the building through my apartment door because I want to dump my stuff and the little folder from the bank so Magnus doesn't see it.

So I'm a little surprised when I come down the stairs and into the ground floor of the store that I don't see Magnus. The sign is still set to open and I frown, sliding behind the counter to the little back room.

He's at my desk, papers and bills in one hand and the other sliding down over the accounts.

For a moment, I can't move as ice moves heavy through my veins. I grip the wall tight. "What are you doing?"

Magnus looks up and swallows, like a kid caught red-handed in a cookie jar.

# Chapter Twenty-One

## MAGNUS

"Zoey, I didn't hear the bell."

"I asked a question."

Her big eyes are filled with something like betrayal and it hurts. Of course, I'm a bastard, a careless, stupid one who just figured I'd hear the bell and be able to put this stuff away.

I have options, and about half a second to decide my course of action. I'm going with something that slides close to the truth and is as far from it as it can be. "Looking at the books."

"I can see that, Magnus." Her voice is closed and tight and I want to smooth that way, but I just put the bills down and fold my hands on top of everything.

She's in bad shape. It could be worse. But it could all be a hell of a lot better. There are about twenty ways right off the top of my head I can think of now that will get her place from her and into my hands.

None of them are good. Most of them will hurt her beyond what I want.

Funny. If I'd been asked that and seen all this before I'd walked into her store pretending to look for a job, I'd have done one of them without even a second thought.

I'm going to stick to the plan I have, though. It's better for her.

She'll still be hurt, but she won't be destroyed.

"I asked a question."

I sigh. "I don't really have an excuse. Except I wanted to see if there was anything I could do to help you. Fair's fair. You offered to help me and..."

Shaking my head, I push my hand through my hair and slowly stand.

"I know what you're thinking," I say, keeping my voice low. "That I looked to see if you really could help me."

"I'm not a fan of you looking, but if you want my help, I'm—"

"Not taking your help, Zoey." It's a simple thing, the con. All you have to do is make them think it's their idea. But I'm not doing that here. The con I have going has to do with dear old gran, yes, but not this right here and now. She'll give me everything. I'll have this place and then I'll make sure Zoey has all the money she needs. Maybe, if I'm feeling generous, I'll buy her a nice place to set up, well, shop.

But first I need to get out of this predicament, and I need to shore up all the other things to do with her building. I need to make sure Lichtenfeld's out of the picture on all the avenues surrounding my project.

"I just worry about you, and I wanted to make sure you can get through."

"Don't."

I move past her and cross the floor to the door and turn the lock and flip the sign. No one's coming in here to buy a last-minute book in the rain. And if they are, they can go fuck themselves. I need to talk with her, to convince her I'm the good guy I'm not.

"While you were gone, someone from Sinclair came by."

"One of the goons?"

I nod, knowing Georgio would hate being called that. Again. For a tough guy, he sure gets hurt by the things sweet Zoey says about him.

Feeling like the goon himself, I pull the crumpled envelope from my back pocket. It's not much, but I happen to know what's there will rock her world in the wrong way. Veiled threats, pressure, the kind of thing that comes with the territory of getting what you want.

"Here. I didn't open it, but I did speak to the guy." And then I say, "From what he said, they can't do much more than try and make you miserable. Legally."

Her shoulders sag as she takes the envelope and squeezes it tight. "They're good at the misery type."

"You could just sell, hold out, make some decent cash."

Zoey's shoulders stop sagging and snap to attention as her violet-blue eyes flash with fire. "Not on your life. That's giving in. I don't do that."

"I know. Which is why I went through the books. I'm sorry."

"That's..." She turns and sets the letter down on the counter, then faces me again and her soft, compact curves and pretty face call to me, do things to me, reach down inside and I want to touch her. So I do. I cross to her and take her in my arms. "That's okay."

"You sure?"

"Yeah."

And I kiss her because her mouth is a beacon and it calls to me. She tastes like rain and sweet spice that belongs to her alone and I wonder if a man can ever get sick of a taste like that? Of the heat and wetness of her mouth that just makes me want to ravish her, here and now and who the fuck cares who can see?

But I lift my head. "Should I go?"

"Probably. It's the sensible option." Zoey slides her hands slowly up my chest, making my muscles heat where she touches. She rises up on her toes to kiss me again. "But this seems a little nicer."

"The better option?"

She links her fingers at the back of my neck and tugs me a little closer. I slide my hands down her waist to her ass and pull her in against my growing erection. "A delicious one."

We head upstairs, her hand in mine. I'm thinking she's going to change her mind, or need a moment. I'm thinking this is the worst idea and the best. Worst because I can get lost in her. Best because it brings us closer together for my plans.

And then she turns when we hit the little hall and she pushes me into the wall, her mouth seeking mine.

I take hers in a deep, hungry kiss and walk her backwards, sliding the zip down her back, pushing the dress and bra from her, freeing her breasts so I can touch them, let them slide against me, and then I unhook her bra, and let it fall along with the dress, tugging that over her hips so I can take her panties with it. And then she's soft and naked in my arms and we're at her bedroom door.

It doesn't take long until we're both naked and breathing hard on the bed. My mouth is all over her. I can't get enough, and she's the same with me. We're burning up, the need eats at me and I don't get it. I don't know why she affects me so much. She's sweet and open and made of a titanium down deep, but it's heated, there's no ice about her. There's no agenda with Zoey.

Sliding my fingers down her body, I push into her and she cries out, biting down on my shoulder and I pump into her, spreading her thighs for me. "You're so wet, Zoey."

"And you're so hard." She wraps her hand around my cock and squeezes, making me groan in the back of my throat.

"Seems like this is a perfect fit." I pull her hand from me, and tease her clit before sliding out of her pussy.

I look down at her, and deliberately suck her juices from my fingers, and she bites her lip. The sight of her, the taste sweet and salty on my tongue is so fucking erotic I could come right here and now.

Instead, I push into her, and take her, pounding into her tight depths like I can't get enough and she eats me up with those big eyes.

Something comes over me, a quiet, ragged fury that's at myself, and the way she looks at me, like I'm the center of this all, so full of fucking trust, I pull out of her. With my hand on her hips, I kneel, moving her, flipping her so her perfect ass is facing me, and I slide my fingers down over her slit, opening her and then I fist my cock, and pump it, and aim. And I slam down home.

"Oh, God. That's so deep. So good." Zoey groans, her hands fisting the covers.

I hold her hip in one hand, and coil her hair in the other, and I fuck her. Hard. Like a madman, and it's insane. Incredible. Hot. She pushes back to meet me, taking me so far into her I don't ever want to emerge.

The weird anger morphs into lacerated need and I pound, sweat dripping, and I pull her head up, and then come over her to bite her shoulder and my balls ache and my body is filling with a pleasure and need for release that borders on pain and her cunt tightens around my shaft, and then she starts to shake. She's coming, I can feel her clamping down on me.

She's crying and moaning and saying things that aren't words and as she screams, her body contracts so hard, over and over on my cock that I explode into her. I'm flying and yelling out because what's inside me, this intense white pleasure is too much to contain.

When I'm done, when she's done, I pull out and collapse on the bed, taking Zoey in my arms and holding her, kissing her, stroking my fingers against her skin like she's the most precious thing in the world.

And I wonder…what the fuck have I become?

I've turned into some kind of weakling when I wasn't looking.

That's the only explanation I've got for having more sex with Zoey, cooking dinner with her. Having more sex.

I sneak out at almost four am, and heading to the apartment I set up for Magnus Simpson.

Laying on the bed in the place, I watch shadows chase each other on the ceiling, but I know sleep isn't going to come along anytime soon, so I pull out my phone and get to work. I answer all the damn texts from my brothers, along with work ones. And I send out instructions for the day to various people for my next phase in my charity and foundation work to show I have heart.

But what I can't do is get rid of the feeling that's building inside me.

It's insidious and uncomfortable and makes things a little darker, like I can harbor real guilt. I don't. I won't. This is all business, and if Zoey is in the way, well, she's going to come out better than she is now.

Whether she likes it or not.

She's rock bottom and she knows it. Oh, she owns the place and she keeps her head above water, so on paper she's in a better position than most. But I can make one or two moves and that head above water thing is going to be a lot more difficult.

If.

The urge is strong and I'm not proud of it, because the urge feels a lot like running away, which is something I don't do.

My plan is best, and I'm going to move things along. All of them.

With that in my head, I close my eyes and let myself drift.

"Boss?"

I pour my third cup of coffee that morning. It's seven a.m and I've had maybe two hours sleep, and Georgio's voice isn't my favorite thing to hear with that little sleep and this early.

"No."

He sighs. "You pay me for my opinion."

"I pay you to obey."

"And for my opinion." He sounds a little wounded. "And I think this means it's prime moving time."

I take a sip of the coffee. "It'll save us a few hundred thousand. We stick to the plan. Just deal with the riff raff hanging about. Properly."

Lichtenfeld will give up with the right pressure, so I'm not worried on that front. What does disturb me, is the, er, illegal information on Zoey's bank account Georgio handed me.

For some reason, it's more depleted than it should be. And she's paid up everything on the place. Ahead of time.

That wasn't in her books yesterday. Still, maybe that's why she took off yesterday, to stay on top of things to stop me trying something underhanded with the bank.

"Just do that, and I'll let you know when we need the next move."

And I disconnect the call, grab my fall coat and head out into the world.

At the store things are fine. And Zoey heads upstairs around mid-morning for something or other.

We haven't mentioned the night before, but it's there, burning between us, making the air taut, alive, thrumming with awareness. But that can stay on the back burner. I prefer it there. I want to have sex with Zoey. I have a horrible feeling I'm going to have to have sex with her for a long time, so while I sort that shit out, I'm more than happy to not mention what happened.

Just like I'm actually happy she's upstairs, out of temptation's way.

"You're an idiot," I mutter.

I'm about to get a coffee when Zoey suddenly screams.

# Chapter Twenty-Two

## ZOEY

"Are you okay?"

Magnus's voice reaches me before he does, and he bursts into the kitchen like a wild thing. And then stops, taking me in. I'm soaked to the bone, a drowned rat. On the floor.

Behind me, water shoots out from beneath the sink.

His mouth is open and I snap. "Bathroom sink. Get the toolbox."

I turn and continue fruitlessly trying to stave off the water with my hands.

"Here." Magnus hands me the box and I fling it open, grabbing the wrench and battling with the stuck water tap. It finally gives and the water slows to a trickle and then stops.

I sag. The water's soaking into the floor and if it drips down through the light fixtures and onto books in the room below I'm in trouble.

"Go and move all the boxes and books in the room beneath."

Magnus doesn't wait for me to clarify, he takes off, and I pull open the drawer with old rags and dump them on the flood. Next come the tea towels. And then I'm up and dragging all the towels I can get my hands on into the kitchen.

I'm in the midst of soaking and wringing into a basin and repeating when Magnus returns. He simply drops to his knees and joins me, making faster work of this than I can.

"Sorry," he says. "I've got no idea about pipes and things like that. Plumbers, however, I can do. One's coming shortly."

I bite down on the groan that rises up. More money I now really don't have, growing wings and flying out the window. But the old pipes have needed replacing for years and I can't live without water. Or live with using just the bathroom sink.

"Thanks."

He puts a hand on my thigh, my jeans almost black from the water. "It's not your fault."

"No, but I know these things are a pain in the ass."

"It'll be okay." Then he gets to his feet and disappears. He's back in a few minutes. "I locked up. The plumber will call me when he's here."

I want to say I'll do it, but turning off the water tap to the pipe in the kitchen is as far as my skills go, and judging from the way Magnus stared like the scene was something out of a horror film, his skills are no doubt less than mine. And, I knew the day to replace the pipes would come.

I'd just hoped it would be down the track, on a day of my choosing. Not from near-disaster necessity.

We continue cleaning up and there's something nice about having him there. I just wish...well, I wish for a lot of things and I can't have any of them.

But it's better than thinking of the pure pleasure last night had been. That's dangerous because that kind of pleasure a girl might want to keep, might want to dream on. Especially when you combine it with the man who's helping you, the man whose complexity and layers call.

"It'll be okay," he says, sitting back on his heels.

I look at him. Tears, hot and blurring, press at my eyes, but I blink them away. "Will it? I know this is bad. And—"

"Hey."

Swiping a hand at my eyes, even though the tears don't fall, I swallow and shake my head. "I don't know why I'm suddenly feeling overwhelmed. I face crap every day. And I don't get all whatever this is."

"You don't need to act like a Valkyrie every waking second to be one." Magnus gets to his feet and holds out his hand, and I place mine in his, letting him pull me to my feet. "Thing is, you're used to taking on the world, but right now, you don't have to."

"Yes, I do."

"It's not going to crumble if you take a moment for yourself. And you're not alone. I might be shit at a lot of practical things you do in your sleep, but I've got strong shoulders."

I just stare at him. If he keeps going, I'm going to be a drowned rat in other ways. Like stupid tears.

"Zoey?" He's smiling, and it's soft and inviting and I want to curl up in its center. Metaphorically.

"I'm okay. I just needed a moment. And now I've had one. I'm just going to get this cleaned—"

"No. You're not."

"I'm not?"

"Nope. You're going to put on dry clothes, then sit on your sofa and have a cookie. I know you want one."

"Ass."

He grins. "That's no way to talk to the man who's going to take care of this watery mess for you. And feed you." He looks about as he grabs the glass cookie jar on the counter and dumps three on a plate. Then he turns to me. "Get changed."

I do, leaving my soaked clothes in the basket in my room and pulling on fresh jeans and a T-shirt, leaving my feet bare. When I go back to the kitchen, Magnus is texting.

I don't know if he sees me, but he finishes and puts his phone in his pocket and picks up an unopened bottle of merlot. Then he looks right at me, like he knows whenever I'm there.

It makes my breath hitch in my throat.

He shakes the bottle at me. "What do you have that's stronger than wine?"

"I don't need a drink." I don't, but now he's suggested it the thought is comforting, almost as comforting as he's being. Like this, a girl could fall head over heels for him.

What am I thinking?

A girl could take one look at him and fall head over heels. This is just the delicious center of the cake beneath the glorious icing.

I push a hand through my wet hair, trying to calm the thud of my heart that's spiking high. "I think there's something in the pantry."

Magnus roots around and pulls out a dusty bottle. "Sherry?"

"It's a thing." I give him a challenging look as he pulls down a glass for the fortified wine. "People pay good money for good sherry."

"Good being the operative word." He unscrews it and sniffs. Then recoils. "Fucking hell. No."

He puts the lid back on and digs around some more, finally pulling out something I'd forgotten about. I think it's vanilla vodka Suzanna once insisted we drink. He sniffs this, wrinkles his nose and shrugs. "This is also bad. But not as bad as the sherry...it'll do."

The amusement in his voice that battles pure disgust warms. He pours me a glass, adds some ice, gives me the cookies, then makes me go to the living room and sit. I feel like some overgrown child, but it's nice, the pampering. His phone buzzes, and Magnus glances at the screen and holds up a finger.

"Everything okay?" I ask. I can't help it. Even with my mini disaster going on, I know there's a lot happening in his life.

"Don't worry." He smiles, flashing his dimple as he goes into the kitchen, clearly talking to his gran. When the plumber comes, Magnus takes care of that, too, letting the guy in and bringing him up here. I know it's going to cost a fortune, but right now I don't let myself go there.

Usually I'm dealing with so much, but right now there's someone helping me. It's both weird and wonderful all at the same time.

And still the anxiousness for him scratches at me. "How is she? Should—"

"Gran's going to bed early; she's fine," he says in that way people do when things aren't fine but can't do anything about them, "and thank you for worrying. But you don't need to."

Magnus doesn't quite meet my gaze when he says that, but there's only so far I can push, so I nod. There are things I can do, and he doesn't have to know about them. But I also need to take care of the pipes.

But I can do it. I can do it all. Help his gran. Keep my building from the hands of the ominously quiet Edward Sinclair and get these pipes fixed.

"Hey. It really is going to be okay."

"I don't want to lose a day...do you think...?" I shake my head, stopping myself because how would he know? "Magnus, I'll make sure everything is fine."

"You're not alone. And the plumber's doing the work needed for now."

"I should go and speak to him. Work out a plan." I set the glass down and start to push up to my feet when he stops me.

His hand is warm on my arm as he does so. "I took care of this."

"You can't." I don't need to ask what he means by that.

"The guy's Gran's neighbor. It's a discount, and..." He shrugs. "It sounds like there'll be other work."

Someone clears their throat and my stomach drops as the plumber comes in to the living room, wiping his hands on a rag. "You'll have water, but those pipes gotta be upgraded soon."

I stand, doing mental calculations in my head. "How long can I put it off?"

"Best case? A few more weeks, maybe a month; but..."

"Yeah, I know." I nod. "Do you have a card?"

The guy reaches into his pocket and pulls out a little flip tin and opens it, handing me a card. "I'll be back tomorrow a.m. You might want to close up until after lunch."

"I thought you said—"

"This is a quick fix. Tomorrow I'll put in a permanent fix for this pipe. But everything will need an upgrade."

I swallow, nodding. "And how much?"

The guy pauses a moment, glances at Magnus.

"How much?" I ask again.

"I'll get you a quote."

After he's gone, I sit and close my eyes.

"Here."

I open them, looking at Magnus's proffered hand. He's holding out my newly refilled glass.

"I'm not sure more booze is going to solve the problems."

"It's not just booze. I ordered pizza." His tone is so serious I almost laugh. "And everyone knows that combination's the sweet spot for problem solving."

Now I do laugh, and put the card from the plumber on the coffee table. I take the glass and he holds the one in his other hand up. "Here's to getting on a new and better road."

"This road is okay," I say, downing my drink. He does the same. "But I'd like better."

"Ask and you'll receive. Or that's how it's meant to go, anyway." He shakes his head, like he's made some kind of decision, and drinks his vodka, and then he goes to the kitchen and comes back with the bottle, sitting next to me and refilling our drinks.

"Are you trying to get me drunk, Mr. Simpson?"

He gives me a long, considering glance, one that smolders in the center and flame licks up inside me. "Do I need to?"

"No."

He leans in, and I want that kiss that burns in his gaze and his mouth comes so close to mine I can taste it.

Of course, that's when the doorbell rings and the tiny moment is shattered. Magnus sets down his drink and gets to his feet. "Pizza."

When he returns and we're eating the pizza, I shake my head and say, "I'm going to pay you back for all this."

"Why?"

"I need to."

His eyes darken. "No, you don't."

"Yes, I do." I set my pizza slice down and pull up my knees to my chin. "You can't afford it, and I'm not built that way."

"What way is that, Zoey?"

I breathe out as he smooths a curl from my face. "The charity way, I can get by on my own."

"Everyone needs a little help, even if it's someone there for them, or a pizza."

"It's just..." I stare at him, those onyx eyes are so warm and inviting. "I've made my own way, and that's one thing instilled in me, you know? Help others where you can, and look after yourself. Clean up your own messes. This is my mess. I let things get like this. I should have—"

"What? Taken care of something big like the pipes when you didn't have to?"

"But I did have to. I knew they were old and—"

"Zoey, unless someone told you this must be done a year ago, five years ago, a week ago, whatever ago; unless someone told you that if you didn't disaster was right there, then you wait until you have to do something. Did they?"

"The last time I had a plumber in, they said one day I should replace all of them, so I knew what that meant."

"Yeah, but they didn't say this would happen. Come on. So you knew one day, but you got by. This isn't your fault."

I sigh and rub a hand over my forehead, but he takes my hand, and lifts it to his lips, kissing my fingers. "Not. Your. Fault."

I could argue it. I'm not stupid. I knew I needed to do something, but I always pushed it back, always figured things would hold on. And maybe he's right.

"We'll think of it tomorrow. You'll have the day off. You won't pay me, because I'll use that time for things I have to take care of, and then we'll get things done. And everything has a way of working out. Maybe not how you want, but things work out. And time always is a gift that shows you things in a neutral light the further along you get."

"Have you been reading the back of cereal boxes?" I ask with a laugh.

"That and the inspirational section of the bookstore. Just the blurbs."

"Idiot."

"Around you? Yeah, I think I am." And Magnus leans in, kissing me, his mouth warm and tasting like pizza, vodka, and that dark moreish taste that's him alone, one that's full of sex and toe-curling things.

The kiss isn't deep, but the passion teases at my edges and inside I shift, a latent need starting to burn as I return the caress, my hands sliding into his hair and it's the sweetest tease, his mouth on mine, his tongue slow dancing, drawing me into him.

Finally Magnus lifts his head. "I could kiss you all night. I could do a whole bunch of other things, but maybe we should just settle down and watch some TV?"

"Are you respecting my taking things slow, even though we've been down and dirty and naked?"

"There's intimacy and then there's intimacy," he says, pulling me in against him as he reaches for the remote control.

I smile against him. It's true. The sex is physical, and that kiss and this? Emotional, and it's also giving me room to breathe.

How the hell did I get so lucky in meeting him?

And what am I going to do when he finally walks away?

# Chapter Twenty-Three

## MAGNUS

"Mag? Magnus? Ed?"

I turn in my chair and glare at Ryder. "Why are you here again?"

"Checking in on you. Kingston's out of town wheeling and dealing, and Hudson and Scarlett are in Europe."

"So you're bored."

"Well..." He spreads his arms to encompass my office, "maybe I wanted to check up on how your task is going?"

"You're bored. And it's going well." Actually, better than well.

The final pieces are ready for my ongoing charities and foundations and they're good. Actually, I'm pleased to have done them. They look good on paper and they feel better, because I'm doing something that'll make a difference.

It's so fucking decent I disgust myself.

Since the pipes at the bookstore were like some kind of gift, my plans there are being fast tracked, too. Although that doesn't have to come at the same time, there's pressure.

The sooner I'm done, the sooner I'm free and the faster I shake the darkness that clings.

Darkness because I'm conning her. She's going to offer to help my fake gran. That's more than obvious. Amelia's done her part by backing up the operation angle and the threat of losing her apartment.

I don't need the money. I'm not going to take it, but the moment she shifts things the right way, we can topple the place from under her and snap it up under a subsidiary. The pipe is icing.

It should be sweeter than what it is.

"What happened to me being the bad guy?"

I give him a narrowed eyed look. "I told you that was just in passing."

"Yeah, yeah, just thought I'd check."

"Don't."

Ryder comes over after studying the plans I have up for the next phase of my dream, and picks up the matte black folder and flips through it.

"All of this...it looks good." He looks me up and down. "So why don't you look happy?"

I sigh. "I'm ecstatic."

"Nothing to do with the little bookstore lady?"

"Leave her out of this."

"I can't. She's your epicenter."

I get up. "She's nothing of the sort. A means to an end."

Those words leave a bitter taste in my mouth, one I'm not sure I can rid myself of. Although that's probably just her goodness rubbing off on me.

"That why you have..." He flips to a page in my folder, slaps it down on my desk and spins it to face me, his finger coming down on the thick paper. "This?"

I look up at him. "I'm not a monster. We've been over this and she's going to be better off without that sinkhole for money. This is my way of doing something she'll like."

"Yeah, but—"

"Did you turn into some kind of saint when I wasn't looking?"

"Hardly. I've got this blonde tonight. Smoking. But...that doesn't change you and this Zoey person. Or what's going on. Because it's sort of veering on evil, Magnus."

Shaking my head, I get to my feet. "Hardly. She'll have more than enough money to set up anywhere she wants after this. I need that spot."

"Yeah—"

"Just like you apparently want your share of the family legacy, a share I'm guaranteeing by proving I've got heart. Now, if you don't mind, we're launching everything this weekend. And then I'll deal with the whole Zoey thing."

"Cutting it close."

"As I said, I'm not a monster, Zoey—"

"Oh, yeah, you're real neutral when it comes to her. I meant the proving you've got heart. Just remember, fires have a way of raging out of control, Magnus."

My brother's words haunt me. All through my meetings, all through the shit I need to do. Even now, through this meet up with Jenson, my dear dead father's attorney.

"This looks fantastic," he says. His face is neutral as he says it, but this doesn't faze me. Jenson likes to play things close to the bone, just like my father did.

I give him a neutral look back as I recline in the old fashioned wine-red chair in his darkly tasteful home office.

The place befits an ivy league educated attorney, one who rubs shoulders with the rich and powerful. One who keeps secrets. One who's from the same world as his clients. The dark polished floors. The built-in teak bookshelves with beautifully bound books. The window that overlooks the tree lined East Sixty-Seventh street address. His big desk that's used as well as something for show.

Jenson's been on the periphery of my life growing up, handling all the things my father needed handling, the private things. Divorces, prenups. All of it.

I've half a mind to ask why and how a man like him, one who knew the intricate details of my father's life, way more than me or my brothers or any wife, has remained close to my mother.

"Is something bothering you?"

"I don't like being jerked around," I say, tapping a hand on the chair's arm. "My brother got jerked around, and the details keep changing. What surprises are coming my way?"

He breathes out and closes the folder. "This meets everything you've been asked to do. This shows, on paper, you have heart. As long as you don't dump it the next day, which..." He pulls his laptop to him and taps something on the keyboard, the screen lighting up and reflecting on his face and gold-rimmed glasses. "I don't think you're going to do unless you want to look like some kind of modern-day scrooge—"

"It's not Christmas."

"—or lose the vast chunk of money you've tied up in all of this. We still have some time left, not much, but it looks good. I'll pass this on, and you'll know on the day. But between us, your stake seems to be set and the family business still in the family's hands."

"It doesn't answer the questions I have as to why he did this."

Jenson folds his hands together. "Your father always had reasons for things."

"I know. Which is why this doesn't make sense." I study him. "Maybe you can tell me why my mother's so interested in all of this?"

Jenson, of course, remained tight-lipped on that. Just an 'ask her', but when Faye wants to be elusive, she's a ghost.

The next morning I need to head in to the damn store. I'd love to say that's done, too, but it isn't.

Zoey has a way of sliding so far into a man that she tangles around him, but this thing with us isn't something I'd ever planned. Not to this point. Not where I like her, where I care. Somewhere what I wanted and how I wanted to do things changed. I still need the building, but in another life, I just might want her, too.

I'm not what she wants, though, not really. She wants a fantasy, someone who doesn't exist. But for the first time, with all my money, I wish I could give her that. And...I can't.

The car I'm in pulls up a block away. It's another morning of gunmetal gray sky that threatens rain and makes colors saturated.

I've done what I can though, I tell myself as I eat up pavement to get to the store. This morning, before I got here, I went over Zoey's finances. She won't be able to hold out against me. That's obvious. The pipe situation, well...I think that and her sudden bank visits to speak to the loans people mean I might be able to back off on the gran thing.

My plan of Zoey giving me money to help with the nonexistent operation is making my stomach more and more knotted.

As I told my brother, I'm not that much of a monster.

But I know Zoey would do it. I suspect that's why she's been visiting the bank.

It's not like I'd keep a cent she gave me. And I was merely going to ask for a few thousand dollars which I know would push her over the wrong colored line, but...I don't think I have to.

I think I'm going to simply take care of everything else and let the destruction fall naturally. It won't be long.

My chest tightens as I push open the door to the store and it's a punch down low when Zoey looks up and smiles.

It's a million dollar kinda smile, I realize, even when there's strain and worry at the edges; it shines. Just like her.

"Hey." I don't think, I just stride across the floor of the store to where she is at one of the bookshelves and I slide my arm around her and brush her mouth with mine.

Warm. Sweet. Soft. Spiced. Inviting. She's all that with a complexity that hides below her surface. I could spend weeks diving into all that. Maybe months.

She sighs. "We shouldn't. We said we'd take it slow."

"I know." I kiss the underside of her chin as I brush the hair from her throat with my free hand. "But you're too delicious."

Her soft laughter is music.

Zoey pushes free, reluctance at doing so all over her face. "I need to run off this morning. But..." She bites her lip. "Can we talk a little later? I wanted to discuss something with you."

My heart starts to beat fast. She's going to offer me the money for fake gran. I can feel it. "Zoey—"

"I should have texted you last night, but I only decided to keep this appointment this morning." She rises on her toes and kisses me, then the bell dings and she stumbles back and to the counter to grab her bag and coat I didn't notice that sit there. "I'll be back in a few hours."

"You want me to man the store?"

She smiles again. "You've done it before. I trust you."

And then, she's gone.

The customer buys a handful of books. They're looking at the area, because of my name linked to the upcoming project. And it's interesting to hear the guy talk. He's like all the well-heeled, looking for a touch of Brooklyn cool, and is saying how he's looking to buy around here because he knows how the prices will skyrocket once the Sinclair project takes off.

People like that... I shake my head as the guy leaves, and I'm not like him. I can see the value of things, while he's just trying to cash in, like Zoey's ex, Bronn.

"Where's Zoey?"

I frown and stop, staring after the guy who left and Mikey stands there, glancing about, a worried expression on his face. "She had errands."

"Oh. Yo, why you talking to that dude?"

"The customer who left?" I prep the little bag of treats Zoey always gives the kid, because he's a little skinny. "I'm meant to do that. You know, the hint lies in the word customer."

The kid glares at me, but nabs the paper bag I set down. "He was talking about that Sinclair dude."

"He's the one behind the after school job you have," I say, somehow keeping the annoyance out of my voice.

Mikey sniffs. "Yeah, but I don't see him. And I'm not with the evil arm." Then the kid looks me up and down in a way I don't like. "How you know him?"

I'm sure there's a terrible sitcom in this. Somewhere. I don't want to get in deeper in my web. I'm the spider, not the fucking fly. So I just say, "He's running a bunch of charities and centers."

"Hard to move in this town for all the rich dudes." Mikey shifts a bit, then shoots a furtive glance about. "Tell Zoey I said hi. Laters."

After he leaves, people come in. Some to buy or browse, but there are a bunch who have lived here for ages, who are moving or getting ready, and they all come in to see Zoey.

And all of them, every single fucking one, have nothing but great things to say about her.

Even Tuesday Harry drops by and the colorful Mrs. O'Reilly who flirts with me in that way happily married older women do—just for fun and no meaning behind it.

They're not moving on...Harry is a few blocks away, but he worries that other developers will move in, and he's right. They will. When I build, prices will skyrocket further. It's the way of the world. I don't say it. I don't say a single word of reason to any of them.

It's not until around four pm that I realize a few things.

One, I actively find myself adoring Zoey the way these people do, and despising their mythical version of Edward Sinclair.

Two, where the hell is Zoey?

Three, I got so hungry I ate a cookie and it was like the entire world switched on. The burst of complex flavors and sugar surge through my blood, which might explain the first thing.

But I don't think so.

It's Zoey.

She's got in deep.

She's made me sit here and dislike Edward Sinclair as though he's someone else.

# Chapter Twenty-Four

## ZOEY

I can't wipe the smile off my face, even though I feel like I've been to hell and back.

And I hate to even dare admit it to myself, but it's because of Magnus. He's in the store, and he looks like he belongs.

It's a fallacy, I know that, but it's hard to tell your heart something like that when it wants what it wants.

Not that I'm in love with him or anything.

But I could.

I could fall. So very easily for him.

With a breath, I push open the door and walk in and his smile with the flash of dimples is enough to ignite my smile all over again and make my knees want to turn into unset Jell-O.

"Everything go okay?"

I nod. "Here?"

For a moment, he has a darkness that comes to his eyes, but it disappears, almost like it was never there. And perhaps it wasn't. "Apart from every single person in the world seemed to come in to sing your praises and some of them left you cards, I think, judging by your suddenly swollen little pile of mail."

And that dark expression is suddenly explained.

People who have to move out came by. No doubt Magnus is angry, which I get. I am, too. Add that to his pride and his unwillingness to discuss the need for money for his gran and the things I know he doesn't, well... "Sinclair is an ass."

"You might find you like him. If you met him."

"I wouldn't. People like that...well, you know about Bronn, and Edward Sinclair's a million times worse."

"Zoey—"

"Magnus, wait a moment." I pick up my mail and somehow resist touching him, resist tracing the lines of his veins on the back of his hand that rests on the counter. Then my gaze falls on the plate with the crumbs. "Did...did you have a cookie?"

He groans. "Four. I had four. I didn't bring a protein bar today for lunch and I got hungry and I think they're the second best things I've had in my mouth."

"What's the first?"

His gaze locks with mine and my temperature skyrockets. "You."

All the air in the room isn't enough. I can't breathe. I fan myself with the mail.

"Sorry, I shouldn't have said that. But it is true."

"Magnus, you—" I shake my head and drag in an uneven breath. "You're dangerous."

"I'm not."

"To women everywhere. To me."

He raises a brow and comes around from behind the counter. He looks down at me, and slides a finger beneath my chin, lifting it. "Is that bad?"

"Yes. No." I can't help it. I trace my fingers along his chest, the heat of him a sweetness against my flesh, a little buzz racing through me from the touch. "You just make it hard to think."

"You said you wanted to talk?"

"Yeah." I want to move away. I'm lying. I want to move closer and draw him down to me and kiss him. "Friday or Saturday I'm going to go to the Catskills. There's an estate sale and some great little stores I want to peruse for books."

"You want me to helm the store?"

"No." The words out before I can think. "Did you want to come with me?"

Magnus said yes.

The thought plays over in my mind. All through the rest of the day. All through my walk over to his gran's.

When she lets me in, the tiredness in her face tells me I'm making the right decision.

"Zoey, dear, Magnus isn't here."

"I know." I take a breath. "I came to see you."

"Is something wrong?"

"No, I have a proposition."

I make her sit and I get us both a cup of tea. As I set mine down on the coffee table, I lean forward.

"Zoey, don't do anything stupid."

"I'm not." I might be, but sometimes stupid is the right thing to do and this feels right. I reach into my bag and pull out the plain white envelope. "I know Magnus is trying to help you and to pay for the surgery. And he won't accept anything from me. But I also know you don't want to leave here. After the surgery, you aren't going to want to be somewhere else, and we're fighting against a common enemy."

"What did you do?" Her hands clutch the tea cup tight.

I smile. "I just did what anyone would do. I went to the bank—"

"No."

"Yes. I went and I have in there a check for you to make out to your landlord. I left that part blank as I don't know what holdings it's under with Sinclair. But if this helps, then I'm happy."

"You tear that up right now. I can't take it. I won't."

"I'm going to be fine." Things are going to be close to the wire and now the patchwork is all done with the pipes and the plumber said we could hold off a number of months and also work out a plan, then I won't lose anything, I can keep everything mine. And this dear old lady won't have her life in upheaval more than it's going to be.

Magnus would say no.

"He can't know about this."

"I can't take it."

I get up. "Tell you what, you think about it and if you truly can't use it, you let me know. And tear up that check. I'm going to be fine."

She's crying and I go over to her and give her shoulder a gentle squeeze.

"Zoey, I can't..."

"You can. You deserve it."

And with that, I leave.

Out on the street, I realize that I'm not far from where Magnus lives. It's only a few blocks. I've never been there, never thought of visiting. I happened to remember it from when he wrote it down along with his number just after he started working for me.

Overhead there's a low rumble of thunder, but the rain that's been threatening to fall all day hasn't yet, so I decide to head over to say hi.

I really don't have an excuse at all. He might not even be there.

But when I press the buzzer, he lets me in.

I climb the two flights of stairs and Magnus is waiting when I get there.

"I don't know why I came here," I say.

And then I kiss him.

His arms come around me as he kisses me back and the need and passion build between us.

We don't say anything as he pulls off my clothes, as I remove his. We just keep kissing and touching each other and he leads me across the small studio to the large bed and he takes me down with him.

This is different. This is soft and sweet and a slow, low burn. It's need that's tangled with emotion.

And, as he parts my thighs and pushes into me, he takes me in measured, almost reverent strokes, like he's savoring every single thrust.

I come up to meet him and I'm swept along on this journey, down into the heated waters that stoke fires and waves and warm me inside out. I could live in this forever, this thing where we're locked together. Him in me, him part of me. Me part of him.

We make love.

An exploration of each other that gets deeper, sweeter, darker, more tangled with every stroke. I don't know where he ends and I begin and I don't want to. All I know is this. All I know is him.

Pleasure builds inside, different from the other times. This is both new and familiar, something that strikes a note I need inside.

I come, shattering in a shower of kisses as Magnus comes too.

And after, we lay there, tangled together.

I slowly drift off in a haze of satisfaction, of being cocooned and held and touched with gentle, loving hands and lips.

And that word, loving, hits me.

I think I might be in love with Magnus Simpson.

# Chapter Twenty-Five

## MAGNUS

That night she came to the apartment plays over and over in my head.

I don't know what drove me to stay there that night. And I'm not sure if it was a good idea or not, but I can't regret what happened when I opened the door. Or the following morning.

I can't.

Time is running out. I know it. Feel it. And I don't mean with the Sinclair jewels or my father's stupid stipulations. Those are pretty much in the bag and if it doesn't work, then I don't see what else I can actually do other than donate a kidney.

The store is something I can't do forever, and since I spoke to Amelia the next day and I have the power over Zoey's building now, there's no reason for me to still go in.

But each day, I've gone in. I'm working hard and not smart since my days are spent with her and the past handful of evenings have been spent at the office or at that apartment, hoping she'll come by again, working on my work moves.

My launch for everything is ready to go. And it's all on paper.

And today? I'm heading out of town with Zoey. Something I absolutely know I shouldn't do. But I can't help myself. I like being around her and—

In my pocket, my phone buzzes so I ignore it as I find a spot for the car. I don't own cars—that's Ryder, but it is a nondescript white one I got from Georgio. It's not his, but I ask and he always gets for me. And a so-called borrowed car is easier to explain to Zoey than me renting one.

The phone rings yet again. With a sigh I press answer and slip the blue tooth ear piece in my ear.

"Mother? I'm busy."

"Where are you? I came by your office and you weren't there. So I ate the cookies."

My hand tightens on the device. Okay, so I might have taken more of Zoey's little baked delights and not given them to my PA. "They weren't for you."

"Homemade and delicious, Magnus," she says.

I ignore her as I head to the store. "Why are you there?"

"Ryder's got himself involved in some kind of scandal. There's a board meeting coming up in a few weeks. Can you help him with this?"

I don't want to know what the latest thing is my brother's got himself into, but it explains his hanging around a little more than usual. Beyond his concern over the jewels and keeping the family company in our control.

But the Sinclair flagship is very conservative in morality in the whole way the business is run. That was my father for you; keep the business as squeaky clean as a church while he himself would dabble in all kinds of things. Namely affairs.

"Is she married?"

"Married and famous."

"Ryder's a little decadent and likes to play fast and loose, but not in business."

"You explain that to the board." Her disappointment lurks beneath the neutral tone. She's had a seat on the board my entire life and not one remarriage of my father's could undo that.

"It's time they brought themselves into this century."

"Magnus."

I sigh as my stomach tightens. Up ahead is Zoey's little store. "Mother, I'm a little distracted, but yeah, I'll talk to him tomorrow."

"Okay." She pauses. It's one of her patented ones. "This all looks good, by the way."

"My project heart."

I can almost hear her wince. "Yes. But..."

"What?"

"There's one part you haven't named."

I know that's not what she was going to say and I know what she's talking about. The centers where kids can go to read and get books and feel safe. Every name I think of doesn't seem right. "Inconsequential."

I ring off, promising I'll talk to my wayward brother. And then I'm there, outside Zoey's place. Before I can hit the buzzer the door opens and she's there, cheeks flushed a pretty pink as she looks up at me. "Oh! I was just coming down to wait."

The smile that blooms inside me is too real, like everything I feel around her. "Wait no more. Your rusted chariot awaits."

She takes hold of my arm. "I can get a car—"

"Zoey." I lift her hand up and kiss her fingers, then I slide my other arm around her waist beneath her coat. "I've taken care of things. Shall we?"

"What about your gran?"

I kiss the side of her cheek. I haven't spoken to Amelia in a couple of days. She's on orders to standby in case I need her. She's well paid, so I don't worry about that. Amelia's done her job. "You want me to bring Gran?"

"No. I'm asking how she is."

"She's good. Now, ready for your trip?"

It's a good day. The trunk is full of books and we poke about various little holes in the wall. I'm a little shocked how much I enjoy it because I'm not doing anything except hanging out with her.

I don't do that. I don't waste time.

Yet here I am, doing exactly that and liking it.

Or maybe it's the company I like.

I'm not the only one. Everyone loves her. From the people at the estate sale to the little stores we go into. A lot know her, some don't, but every single one of these people glow when they talk to her.

If I could bottle that Zoey essence, I'd be a trillionaire.

She pokes me in the ribs as we pull up at a little diner. "You're quiet."

"I had a good day."

I lead her in and the waitress gets us a table. Over burgers and fries—things I don't usually eat—she tells me all about the different people she knows here, and how she loves these trips, and it warms me from somewhere deep in my chest.

Zoey smiles, those dark blue eyes shining. "You're the first person I've ever asked on one of these trips." She shrugs and drags a fry through a dollop of ketchup on the edge of her plate. "It's not Suze's thing, and there's no one else I thought might like it."

"I'm honored."

"It's just a boring buying trip." She rolls her eyes.

I steal the fry from her before she can eat it and I vaguely wonder what I've become. Fries, burgers, cookies, feeling weirdly squishy inside? One might think I have an actual heart. Or maybe one might think I really like Zoey more than I can admit.

That doesn't matter. How I feel or don't feel doesn't matter. This all has a use by date that's fast approaching. And even if I suddenly wanted to do a three sixty, I can't. Her store is slap bang where I'm building.

The best I can do is make the transfer easy, pay her out above and beyond and look back on this all as something sweet, something better than a stupid jewel.

She's going to be fine. I know that. Zoey won't have her crumbling store, but she'll have something bigger, better, that comes with a nice fat cushion of money to fall back on.

I don't know who I'm trying to convince here. Me or the imaginary Zoey of the near future.

"Actually," I say, "it isn't. Because it's with you."

I mean those words. With Zoey, things are better.

I'm going to have to start easing out of her life. I'd prefer it if she never knew who I was. If I didn't spoil that. Already a part of my mind is working on graceful ways to get out of it. Maybe Magnus Simpson and Gran can move because he gets a job. Maybe he can convince Gran that moving is better than staying.

But I'm not going to think about that. I'm going to make sure we have a good time for the rest of the week, and then I'll disappear.

"I'm glad you're here, Magnus," she says quietly. "I like you. A lot."

"I like you."

"I was thinking, maybe...maybe we could see where this goes?" She stops, looking horrified. "Or maybe—"

"We take it one day at a time. See where it goes."

Those are stupid words, I know it, but the softness to Zoey is worth it. The way she doesn't seem so stressed here is worth it. One little lie. One little fantasy. It's not much. And she's into someone who doesn't exist. Someone who is me, but without all the shit she hates. Someone without the fortune and the hard fucking lines I take, the relentless drive.

I didn't even know this Magnus existed until I met her.

"That's a deal," she says.

The drive back to Brooklyn is long, but it passes quickly, and I beg off staying the night, although I spend a little too long making out with her like some kind of hormonal teen.

As I leave, I turn my phone on and I go through the messages from Georgio. I call Ryder, who isn't answering. With a sigh, I tell him to put his dick back in his pants and clean up his act. Then I realize something.

I left a message for Amelia this morning and she hasn't called me back.

She always calls me back.

I'm close enough so I head over there.

The building, I think, really does need an overhaul, and I mentally put it on my list of things to do.

I knock on her door and all along the hall noises tumble out of the other apartments. But Amelia's is silent.

I knock again. "Amelia?"

No answer.

I have keys and she told me she'd be staying there during this. But maybe she's out. So I send her a text and then I unlock the door.

The apartment is dark and silent as I step inside to leave her a note. Hey, she's on my dime. A lot of my dimes, so I don't care about coming in here. I switch on a light and freeze.

It's not just silent because she's not here tonight.

Every last trace of her has been erased.

Amelia Johnson, fake gran, is gone.

# Chapter Twenty-Six

## ZOEY

Reality always returns with a bang or a whimper. Whatever. It always returns. And it can't keep the warmth inside me from wanting to burst open.

I haven't seen Magnus since I got back. That's not unusual since it's the weekend and I'm sure he's spending time with his gran. I know he is, because…he called me last night.

For a moment I wondered if he had something he wanted to say, but instead it was one of those conversations that meandered over everything. Like dreams, and I told him I'm living it.

The bookstore, he'd said.

I agreed but as I snuggled down in my bed, listening to the low, rich cadence of his voice against my ear, I meant more than that.

Even if this thing with him is fleeting, it's a dream.

That's something I'll never tell him.

Magnus doesn't belong in my life, at least not the way he is. I know he has hopes and dreams like everyone else, even though all he said was he wanted to make sure those he cared about were happy, would lead full lives, he's not made to work in a store.

But my stupid heart hopes there will be room for the two of us.

Room in whatever his next adventure will be for maybe a chance.

That's all I want.

I'm an idiot. But that hopeful idiocy is something I won't let go of. Just like I won't stop fighting the injustice of Edward Sinclair.

I sit at the little desk in the back even though the store is open. It's too early for people to come in, and I turn on my computer. Amanda, his gran, never got back to me, not that she had to, so I log onto my account.

She took the money. Check deposited and the warmth in me rises.

The move is a risky one because it puts my business in a precarious situation, but only I know that. And it's doable as long as I keep things on an even keel.

The bell on the door dings and I rush out.

The man coming over to the counter grins. "If I knew that smile waited, I'd have worn my best uniform, Zoey."

"Thanks, Hank." I take the bundle of mail from the postman and we make small talk for a minute until he has to continue on his route.

I hate standing around, so I set the mail down and start collecting the books in the box I have out to put on the shelves. And while I do it, I try not to think about the time as it ticks.

But it's hard because with every passing minute, I keep thinking he's not coming in.

When the bell rings again I whirl, but it's Harry, who looks past me to the cookies with a hopeful expression.

"How are you today?"

"Still no rain, so things ache."

"I hear you," I say as I pick out the new knitting book I found in the sale. It's the perfect thing, full of designs his wife would have made and I know he'll enjoy spending time going over it. I place it on the counter and then slide it into a bag, and add a selection of the chocolate gingerbread and spiced orange and macadamia cookies.

He pulls out his wallet and goes to open it, but I stop him.

"My treat, Harry."

"I'll get you next time," he says, drawing himself up to his full height. "Here, how bout I give you today's paper?"

"Sounds like a deal." I place the folded up newsprint on top of the mail.

"Where's your boyfriend?"

My cheeks start to heat. "He's not my anything. And he hasn't come in yet."

"He's a good one. If he isn't, I'll kick his behind for you."

Harry winks and then makes his way out of the store.

I pick up the paper and my eye catches the headline.

Sinclair Scandal it says. I half glance at the story and the blurry photo, but it's about Ryder Sinclair and I just don't have the stomach for it. So I ignore it.

The bell dings loudly as the door flies open and my heart's already beating like a wild thing as the pressure suddenly changes and even as I turn I know who's there.

Magnus.

I look at him.

And forget how to breathe.

I've seen him naked, I've seen him clothed and wet, I've seen his clothes and dry and all of those are drool worthy. But this…

Oh boy.

Magnus Simpson is in a suit. It's a dark gray suit, like deep charcoal, with a hint of warmth in its center. It is beautifully cut, even if the tie's askew and his hair looks like his hands have worried it too much. He looks drawn and lack of sleep is etched on that beautiful face and I still can't breathe because he's the most devastating man I've ever seen in my life.

Like this, he looks like a stranger.

Except his eyes.

They're worried, but they hold heat and intimate secrets lovers share and I know he's moving on.

"My phone died. I'm sorry, I thought I'd be in earlier than this. I thought I'd be able to get changed."

His words wash over me and I swallow. "Magnus, you…"

"Are you okay, Zoey?"

"You're the one who looks like he hasn't slept."

He laughs softly. "You always think about the other person, don't you? Never you? How the hell have you survived so long?"

"Tenacity?"

He comes over and brushes my lips with his, then reaches over the counter for the charger and plugs in his phone.

"Zoey, we need to talk."

"You had a job interview, didn't you?"

"The suit." He closes his eyes a long moment, then looks at me. "I'm—"

"It's okay. It's good. Expected," I say, the words rushing out.

"Zoey."

I put on my brightest smile. "If you need to work here part time, that's good."

"You'd do that for me?" He asks, after a moment.

I nod. "Of course. And if you want to do that, or don't want to work here, well, that's good, too."

"Monetarily?"

It's the truth, it's a lie, and the things I want to say are all jumbled up inside me. I've budgeted to have him, and I know I need someone to help, but maybe more part time like I first thought. But I don't want him to go and I don't want to hold him back, either. For reasons that have zero to do with money. I just nod.

Marcus touches my cheek. "I've never met anyone like you, Zoey. And...yeah, it was a job interview. Something that'll help with gran, and give me time. But I can still be here with you. If I get it."

I nod again as I realize what he's said.

He wants to be with me. Spend time with me.

I'm not just falling in love with him.

I have fallen in love with him.

Magnus pulls off his tie and shoves it in his pocket. "Let's get to work."

I'm used to him here. I'm used to him in my life. It's fast and it feels right and the shadows in his eyes make sense because he was worried over telling me about the job interview.

I pick up the pile of mail and the paper and they slip a little when I see the dreaded Sinclair name again. This time it's on an envelope, but Magnus is frowning at it and takes it.

"It's probably more empty threats," I mutter as a customer comes in and he just takes the little pile from my hands and disappears into the back a moment.

When he comes out, there's something a little different about him. The suit, no doubt. He looks out of place in my shabby bookstore in that outfit. I ring up the sale and he's turning the envelope in his hands.

I snatch it from him and rip it open and pull out the sheet of paper, but Magnus takes it from me, his gaze scanning it. And he frowns, then looks at me. "Do you trust me?"

"What?" I reach for it but he holds it up high. "Give me that."

"No, Zoey. I asked a question."

His words are quiet, but there's something deep inside them and I stop, dropping my hands to my sides.

"Yes, of course. But why?"

He taps the piece of paper against his palm. "Because I can deal with this."

"I don't know what this is."

"It's from EMS—"

"Sinclair the bully."

"—about the work they did. It's a charge, but I think I have an in."

I frown. "What kind of in?"

My blood turns cold. Is he applying for a job with them? I mean, he can do anything he wants, obviously, but after all this, that feels like a betrayal.

"Just an in."

And then I remember the job he helped Mikey get. "The charity angle, you know someone there."

"Something like that. C'mon Zoey, let's finish the day, I'll do this and then I'll take you to dinner. Somewhere small."

I'm humming even though I shouldn't be, even though something nibbles at the edges because I have a horrible feeling he's going to get the job. And that makes me a bad person, doesn't it?

Bad because even though I'm happy for him, I don't want him to go, and he will.

"But that doesn't mean out of your life, Zoey."

No, it doesn't and he was so sweet and wonderful all day. The man is complex, layered and I know I could spend a lifetime with him and never get bored.

I smooth my fingers down the dress I'm wearing. It's a simple thing, flattering, with flouncy material in a dark blue dotted with black. And I even slip on heels and a little lipstick.

It's probably overkill, but I want to look good for him. I want to feel pretty for me, too, and this time, I can admit it.

I check my phone and he'll be here, soon, so I grab my bag and light coat and fly down the stairs and almost run into a man who's lurking on my doorstep.

It's not Magnus.

Tall, yes; handsome, yes, but in that pretty boy way that's boring; blond.

The last man I expected to see and while not the last one, just one I don't care about. "Bronn?"

He smiles the million-dollar toothpaste smile that melted me when I was young and naïve. Now it does exactly zero. "Babe—"

"Zoey," I say, clutching my bag, wishing Magnus were here, "is my name. Not babe."

"It's been a quick minute." He takes a step towards me like I'm going to melt on him now. And quick minute? More like a quick number of years, but I keep that to myself.

"I'm actually busy, and I'm going to assume this isn't a social call."

"It can be both." He gestures to the store. "I'm here with a proposition. I know Sinclair's buying up everything and has a big project for this block, and I also know you're the one in the way. For a price, I can make you so much money, and—"

"I'm going to stop you there. I'm not interested."

Bronn's gaze slides past me and his eyes narrow. "And I see why."

"What are you talking about?" I turn and see Magnus standing there. He breathes in and starts coming towards us slowly.

Bronn nods with his chin. "You already sold. To Magnus Sinclair."

The entire bottom drops out of my world.

My lips are numb as I try to form words, but I can't.

"Of course you did. Magnus Sinclair gets everything."

I stare at Magnus. It's Simpson. But then I lock eyes with him.

EMS.

Edward Sinclair.

Edward Magnus Sinclair.

That's what I'm betting.

I can't breathe. I can't think.

"Zoey."

It's the way Magnus says my name that does it.

"Oh, God. You're him. Edward Sinclair."

# Chapter Twenty-Seven

## Magnus

F uck.

My entire world rocks and not in the good way. The expression on Zoey's face rips a hole inside me, one so large I don't know how the hell I can heal it.

"Zoey? Are you seeing this guy? It's gotta be a scam. He's out of your league."

My gaze snaps to Bronn and deadly fury stalks through my veins. "Get the fuck out of here, Lichtenfeld. You know exactly zero."

"Yeah, right, I'm not going anywhere."

My hand balls into a fist. I'm ready to punch the asshole's lights out. Not because he gave me away, although that's a good reason—Zoey would have found out eventually, even if my plan tonight had worked out—but because he actually dared say she wasn't good enough.

Zoey Smith is better than me and Bronn put together. She's better than most people I've met and I already feel like dirt for what I have to do. This dickwad doesn't need to make things worse by making her feel worse.

A voice in the back of my head says I've done that myself, but I ignore it.

"Go, Bronn. I need to talk to him."

The steel in her voice is cold and implacable and even an idiot like Bronn recognizes it. "Fine," he mutters. "But if you haven't signed anything, give me a call—"

"Go."

Once he leaves, she just stares at me. It's a look I know will haunt me for years to come.

Not the ice and hate and disgust there, but the pain. The shattered trust, the shattered belief in me, and worse, in herself. All that is there. And I did that. I put that there.

I reach out for her, but she recoils and I drop my hand.

"Oh, my God. I'm an idiot. How much did you laugh at me? And that letter? The one I stupidly trusted you with. Was that just a lie?"

"No. I went to take care of it. You shouldn't have been sent that. Zoey," I say, keeping my voice quiet and even. "Can we go inside? We're on the street and—"

"You think I'm going to invite you into my place?"

It's pretty much mine now, because of the nature of her equity loan. And my finagling. But I keep that to myself because I'm a fucking bastard of the most selfish kind and there's no way out of this. Billions of dollars for one small business she can open elsewhere? With a bigger wad of money cushioning her?

I don't even know why she took the damn loan, since I didn't go through with the Gran con for the imaginary operation. Cold feet. Weak. Call it what you will, in the end, I simply couldn't do it to her.

"Zoey?"

"No. You don't step foot in my life again. I don't care if I starve to death. You won't get this place."

"That's not how things work and you know it." I stop and take a breath. I need to stick to my track. "I was going to tell—"

"If you say tell me who you are, I'm not going to believe you."

I shove a hand through my hair. "No, I wasn't going to do that. I didn't want to hurt you."

"Coward."

"Excuse me?"

"I said you're a coward." She swallows hard and her eyes shine like she's going to cry but no tears come. Zoey is made of stronger stuff than that. "You weren't going to tell me because you wanted to leave looking good, knowing I'd feel bad for you and your gran and just hope you both had a good life and..."

Zoey trails off as her eyes widen. "I'm an even bigger moron than I thought. She's not your gran, is she?"

"No."

"And I— I gave—" Now she closes her eyes and something cold and dark streams through me because that empty apartment flashes in my head. I close the gap between us and take hold of her shoulders, ignoring the flinch and her attempt to pull free.

"Zoey," I say, "this is important. What did you do? What did you give Amelia?"

She laughs and I don't think I've ever heard such a bitter and harsh sound come from her mouth. "It's not even Amanda. I'm too stupid to live. That's what they say, isn't it? About idiots like me?"

"What did you give her?"

"Played into your plan."

"You were never meant to give her anything. What did you do, Zoey?"

"I gave her money to pay her back rent."

"Fuck me." She pulls at me and this time I let her go. "Can you get it back?"

But I know what she's going to say.

"You know I can't because she gave you that money."

"She didn't. She scammed us both. She was meant to be a sympathetic ticket." One I was going to use to con Zoey, but I keep that part to myself. "I need to go, but I'll be back."

"No. Don't come here. Don't call me. Don't do anything."

And with that, she turns and unlocks her door, slamming it in my face.

I want to bang on the door. I want to break it down and make her listen, even though I know I have no right.

No right, and it's not going to change a damn thing. I can't save her place, but I can get her damn money back. I pull out my phone and call one of my cars.

It's after midnight in my office and I've got Georgio working on the Amelia situation. Fuck. I can't believe the old broad scammed Zoey. If she hadn't targeted someone like Zoey I might actually respect her.

She scammed me, too.

I work through the night and by seven a.m. there's a team tracking her down. When you have the kind of money I do, conning a woman I care about is beyond stupid. I'm getting the money back. And it will be soon.

At eight, my mother comes into my office. "I don't know why I have staff."

"They wouldn't dare stop me, Magnus, and you know it."

I shoot her a look as I half close my computer. "Yeah, I noticed that."

"It's a gift mothers have."

"Why am I suddenly your favorite son?"

She laughs. "I wouldn't say favorite, but Kingston's out of town, Hudson and dear Scarlett are on some kind of second honeymoon, and Ryder..." The humor fades. "Ryder's in a whole lot of trouble. I thought you were going to speak to him."

"I can't work miracles, and I did. He likes being a player, and it doesn't hurt anyone."

"There's a husband out there who thinks differently."

I don't have time for this. I stand up as my phone buzzes. Georgio with a text. But I shrug as I glance at my mother. "According to Ry, they're separated and this is publicity between the couple. They're using him to further their time in the limelight. She's famous, the husband—" I stop. "Ryder's a lot of things, but he doesn't lie. And his business is going from success to success. Even if it wasn't, that's his issue, no one else's."

"Yes, but that's not my concern. It's the board and there's that meeting."

"Is it today?"

"It's a last minute one today. You're going to have to represent your brothers."

Shit. "Fine, whatever."

My phone buzzes again. Another message. I pick it up but my mother crosses over to me and puts her hand on my arm. "You're not going to ask about the Sinclair jewels or the board?"

"If Jenson and his little team turn about and say I haven't shown heart, then there's nothing else I can do. I'm not about to denounce everything I own and I'm a little late and a little too atheist to join the priesthood, so..."

"I think you're going to prove that, but sometimes real heart isn't quantifiable."

I click on the phone and my heart suddenly speeds up. "Mother?"

"Why don't I like that tone?"

"You're going to have to represent us all. I have somewhere to be."

I take a deep breath as I knock on the door some hours later.

Leaving my mother to deal with things doesn't bother me. This does. Right here, right now.

No one answers, but I know she's home and I knock again. Louder. More instant.

Finally locks click and chains rattle and the door opens.

She's all dolled up, a million miles both in distance and in appearance to how I last saw her.

I lean against the door jamb, placing my foot strategically to make sure if she tries to slam it she can't.

"Hello, Amelia," I say to the old lady. "I think we need to have a nice long talk. Don't you?"

# Chapter Twenty-Eight

## Zoey

"He's a bastard."

I don't have the energy to smile at Suzanna the next morning. "Go to work."

"No! I'm taking a personal day. And I'll take a personal week if I have to. You need me."

"It's over," I say. "This place. My store. And I know you hate it, but..."

"You love it." She scoots over on the sofa to me and hugs me, cushion I'm holding and all and my eyes burn.

"I can't believe I was taken in by Edward Sinclair."

"I can't believe I never recognized him. Though come to think of it, I don't think I've ever seen a picture of him. They're rich as God, but they don't flaunt it. Except, you know the brother currently on all the gossip sites and papers." She sighs and pushes past the bottle of Jack she brought over last night to find the water. She pours some into a glass and hands it to me. "I don't move in those circles."

"I don't either. I'm an idiot. A fool. I'm everything people roll their eyes at and whisper about behind their backs." I pick at the edge of the cushion, blinking back the burn and the blur.

The last thing I'm going to do is cry over that bastard.

I never told Suze how far it went with him, only the kisses and I'm not going to. But I'm betting she's guessed.

Being a good friend, however, she's not going to say a word. But it's there in her eyes as she looks at me, the knowing I harbor huge feelings for a man who doesn't want them. A man who doesn't deserve them. A man who manipulated me like I was made of the world's softest clay.

I shouldn't have done it. Not the falling in love with him...or the fantasy I created. And not the giving his fake grandmother money. Something I did on my own because I thought she needed it. He set that up with her. Except...except...his reaction said there was more to that than I thought.

It doesn't matter.

Nothing matters except I've lost the store.

It's not in writing. It's not even being whispered, but that money being gone, him who he is, and the loan means he's getting control.

"You can't give up."

I look at Suzanna. "Did you just tell me not to give up?"

"Yep. He doesn't own this place. You're the one thing that stands between his making some more money he doesn't need and not doing that. Don't give in."

"I don't want to, but he—" I stop. "It doesn't matter if I try and stand up, he's going to eventually win. And I don't want to see him anymore."

She stands up. "Get your things. We're going to close up the store and you're coming to stay with me for a bit. That way you can just think."

What else am I going to do? Everywhere I look in here reminds me of him and what we did. What an idiot I am.

"Okay."

Two days later and I know I have to do something. Like go back home and start packing. I've run the entire gamut of emotions. From wallowing to queen of revenge. The last is utterly tempting.

I could be as soulless as him. Fight him dirty, do everything I can to ruin him.

But really, what can I do? This isn't Victorian times. And he's an honest to God billionaire, something that makes me sick to my stomach.

I don't know who he is at all, that's the thing. I don't know who I fell in love with. A construct, yes, but there must have been parts of the real him there.

Thing is, I don't know how that changes anything. It doesn't. Not one thing. The man is a scoundrel, a liar. A player.

Magnus or Edward or whatever his damn name is could have been completely open and honest about every part he showed me and he'd still be the man who shattered my heart, the man who came into my life with the express purpose of scamming me.

It seems cruel, that's what it seems. A cruel thing to do. He makes all those love songs that bleed sadness a walk in the park.

How can I both hate and love him and not know who he is all at the same time?

Suze is at work and I haunt her place.

I've missed about twelve calls from Magnus. And ten identical texts telling me to call him.

With a sigh, I make my way out of Suzanna's West Village apartment and to the Fourteenth Street and Eighth Ave subway to grab the L. I take the train to my Bushwick stop and breathe in the familiar air. It's still threatening to rain, but it's warmer today as I hurry to my store. I have the key in the lock for the apartment entrance when I freeze.

Every single sense in me is on high alert.

I grip the key tight, my fingers turning white. But I've done enough running away. Slowly, I turn and look up.

Magnus.

"Is it Edward? Or do you prefer Mr. Sinclair? Perhaps Asshole Supreme?"

He's as devastatingly gorgeous as ever, and I study him, looking for the truth, but he just looks like Magnus. The jeans and cashmere sweater are beautiful, and look like they cost a fortune. But maybe that's just me looking for the arrogant, evil billionaire lurking in the fantasy I fell for.

"I hate Edward. Magnus is what everyone calls me. I'm guessing Asshole Supreme is used behind my back."

I'm not going to laugh. It's not funny. Because he's destroying what's left of my heart with that rich low voice, that current of complexity that was always there.

"I'm the same person, more or less," he adds, like he can read my mind.

"Go away."

"Yeah, I figured that would be next. I can't. Zoey, we need to talk."

"You stole from me."

"That was Amelia. And I wasn't planning to steal. I'm planning to make sure you have more than enough. But you know there's no way you'd be able to hold out."

I nod slowly. My throat is tight and aching from the effort it takes not to fall apart. He doesn't get that. "I can try and make life difficult. I could take all this to court—"

"I'd win."

The sad regret in his voice riles me. "I'm aware. But I'm betting you never took it that far to where I'd try and fight you in court because I might be able to tie all this up for a long time."

"Zoey, what if shit is just that, shit. It's not happening. It didn't. And I know you."

"You think I'm a pushover?"

"The opposite, actually, but you're a good person."

"Fuck you, Edward."

He stares at me because I'm not a big swearer. But I really don't care right now. I hate him. I love him.

"Zoey, I needed to talk to you and you wouldn't pick up, so if you give me a few minutes, I'll get out of your way."

"You deserve nothing from me. And you think I want a big pay out? You know I don't. You lied to me. For some reason, you decided the best option for getting what you wanted was to come into my life and toy with me and my emotions."

"I came into your life because I wanted to understand you, see what the best approach was."

I shake my head. "That's a lie. You did it to find a weak spot. Tell me, was it horrible having to lower yourself by sleeping with me?"

He recoils. "No. I didn't. You and me, that was real. I didn't mean to be like that. I didn't mean to get involved. But I did because you're you. Every single thing I said to you was the truth. About you. About how I feel about you. That was all real. And trust me, it would have been way easier if I didn't like you. If you hadn't gotten beneath my skin."

Magnus takes a breath.

"So...what? You're suddenly going to wave your wand and let me keep this place?"

"You can't afford the upkeep. And this whole area is set to change."

"You're everything I said you were, Magnus. Evil. Greedy. Uncaring. Money isn't the only thing in the world and you have more than enough. You think you can fix things by giving me money? I don't want money. You know who always dreamed of a bookstore, who shared her love of books with me? My actual grandmother. A real person. She didn't have much. No one did in my family, but she held it together. And she taught me to believe in my dream. All my memories are imprinted in this place and that is worth more than all your billions, Magnus."

"Zoey, things move on."

"How like a man who has no heart."

He doesn't smile as he looks me up and down. "I have one. Pumping blood. And you—"

"You know what, Magnus? You can steal this from me. Scam my money, but Helena Smith, my grandmother, is worth a billion of you and if I didn't hate you so much I'd feel sorry for you."

"Damn it, Zoey," he says, moving up to me. "I'm trying to tell you I'm sorry."

"I don't need that from you."

"Here." He hands me an envelope. "It's the money from—"

"I don't care."

And before I can stop myself, I squeeze my hand into a fist, and I punch him in the face.

He's so shocked he falls down and I crush the envelope in my other hand as the pain of hitting him ricochets up my arm.

"I never want to see you again, Magnus. You win."

And with that, I turn on my heel, rush to my door and unlock it.

Once inside, the lock turned, I start to shake. And I give into the burning tears inside me as I slide down to the ground, the tears falling.

I hate him. I never want to see him again.

All that is true.

Just like the fact I still love him.

I don't know what I'm going to do.

# Chapter Twenty-Nine

## MAGNUS

"Whose fist did you run into?" Ryder asks the next morning.

I rub a hand on my chest, where I hurt. Where I haven't stopped hurting since everything whet to hell. "A girl."

"Oh. Oh, how the mighty fall."

When Zoey punched me, I wanted to laugh. There was nothing remotely funny about it and there still isn't, but the fact she had the stones to do that is admirable.

Everything about her is admirable.

And I screwed up. I know it.

Ryder holds up the new plans I've made, the ones I stayed up late into the night with tequila as my companion doing. I've had them printed and bound and I asked my brother to look at it. Something I never do.

Until now.

Funny how an ache in your chest and the quiet knowledge you screwed up massively can undermine confidence.

"Has she seen this?"

I'm about to say who, but Ryder isn't an idiot. Even without the bruise on my cheek and my saying it was a girl, he'd guess.

"No, I don't think she wants to see me."

"Well, if it were me, I wouldn't either."

I point at him. Playing our games is easier than giving into the anger and pain that stalks my veins. I can separate myself from them because inside it's not done with Zoey. It won't be done until I let her know the plans.

"You've changed, Ry."

"Being played the way I was has that effect." Then he narrows his eyes. "Are you playing her with this?"

"Of course not."

"Is it a game to win her or do you mean it?"

"You can go fuck yourself, Ryder. I did this for her."

"Or," he says, "you did this to make yourself feel better."

"I know she'll like it."

"Is that enough?" My younger brother, the one who can't keep it in his pants and doesn't want to, is suddenly acting all mature. I suspect he's playing his own game because we're still waiting to hear how the emergency board meeting went. But then again, the family company means the most to him. And...

And I'm distracting myself. "You mean is that enough as in what I've done? The answer is yes. And the answer to the other question is this. Of course she'll like it, Ryder."

"Of course," he says. "But are you willing to accept it if she won't take you back?"

"I'm not trying to get with her. We're from different worlds. And she's not my type."

My brother sighs. "I don't know her. But I know you and you don't have a type. It's an anti type. Women who don't mean anything beyond the sexual relationships."

"Some of them are friends."

"This Zoey, you like her. Some might suspect you love her, Mag. And if you're doing this to play a game to get her, then you're going to lose."

"This is a little pot and kettle."

"I know who and what I am. I play. But I understand people."

I snatch the folder from my brother. "You're wrong."

And I head to the door. I might say wrong, but I've a horrible feeling he could be right.

***

Zoey's little bookstore is open when I get there. I walk in and glance about. She's staring at me and if stares from her right now were daggers, I'd be a bleeding, bloody mess on the floor.

No one else is here, so I quickly flip both the lock on and the sign to closed and approach her quietly and carefully.

"You gave me money."

Shit. I forgot the envelope. I rub a hand over my eyes. "Yeah."

"I don't want money from you."

"It was your money."

"From you."

I come to a stop at the counter and place the folder on it. "I handed you the money, that's true, but it's the money you gave that old scam artist. I tracked her down and got it back from her. I'm sorry, that was never part of it."

"Is that all?" She nods toward the door. "You can go now. I have a store to run until I move away."

Those words slice through me. "You're planning on moving from this part of Brooklyn?"

"It's none of your business. I'm none of your business. You won."

I slide the folder to her, but she doesn't touch it.

"Thing is, I don't think anyone's won. I didn't set out to hurt you. But I knew you would and for that…shit, I wouldn't give me a chance."

"You're asking for a chance?"

The disbelief in her voice cuts even deeper into me, and that ache in my chest starts to roll through my blood. Am I? "Probably. I don't like losing,

Zoey. I'm ruthless, and I don't let anything get in the way of what I want. Thing is, I never realized one thing I'd want is you."

"Don't lie to me. It's not fair. You're taking everything and now you're trying to take what? My heart, too?"

I'm doing that, I know I am, and my brother is right, my reasons here are selfish, but he's also wrong, because I want a chance with her, and I think if I work at it, I can get it. But I also want her to be happy. I want to give her what she wants. And I've found a way to do it.

She shouldn't want to see me again, I know that. Yet here I am, taking a risk, a big risk, because I don't know how it will play.

If I lose her. I lose everything.

"I had an epiphany last night. I care because you do."

"You've said I can't win."

"No one wins with my first scenario. As I said, I'm ruthless. I came up with something else." I nod to the folder. "This is the new vision. One where you keep your place. I build around it and... Just read it. Or don't. If you prefer the money, then I've left what I'll pay you in there. And I can go higher."

"Is this to get me back?" She starts laughing and shakes her head, her hands spreading out on the plans and everything I've laid out, page by page. "That's ridiculous. You don't—"

"Yes."

It hits me, how I really feel about her. Why I kept sleeping with her. Why I wanted to spend time with her. Why I enjoyed it. Why she makes me feel like I have a heart that isn't there to just push blood around and keep me alive.

"Yes, Zoey. If there's a chance, any chance at all, yes. But also if you don't want me, can't forgive me then..." I swallow. "Then this will still go through. You being happy means everything to me. So I figured, as you kept pointing out, I'm fucking rich. I can use that money to set aside apartments at prices for the people who still want to live here. I'll build around your store. I'll keep some places, businesses. I'm going to change the landscape, but you're right, these people who want to live here can and should. And if I'm going to change the future of urban living, then I need to look at a bigger picture. And you made me do that."

"Magnus, I don't know what to say." She's big eyed, full of distrust, hope, wariness. I can't see hate, but I'm not exactly looking that deep.

Then again, it's Zoey.

Hate isn't natural to someone like her.

"Don't say anything. Just look at it. My offices are listed on there. And you have my number. Thing is, I've gone and fallen in love with you, Zoey. I never said that. I never realized until everything fell apart. I'm not a great guy, I know that. But you make me better and…well, I hope to hear from you."

And then I do one of the hardest things in my life.

I walk away.

My meetings are done for the day and I haven't heard from Zoey. Did I really expect to?

"Magnus?"

Shit. I realize my mother's been in my office, talking to me for a number of minutes now, and I barely noticed.

"What?"

"I was saying that I'm here unofficially on official business. Your time is up and you showed you have heart. To Jenson and his people, anyway. You met all the requirements laid out by your father."

She hands me a small box and an envelope.

I toss them both down on my desk and tap my finger against the top.

"The contents of the envelope are something you might need to discuss with your brothers. It's to do with the meeting."

Ryder and his fucking the wrong women. Jesus, those people on the board are puritans, but if I passed the test, then they can't do anything. I'm not worried. They can stew or resign and sell their shares. I really don't care.

Then I look at my mother. "So my foundations worked? Showed them I have heart."

She smiles. "Zoey."

"Excuse me?"

"Your test passed because you changed all your plans for Zoey. Congratulations, Magnus. You did it because of her."

A small noise catches my attention and I swing my gaze to my office door.

Zoey stands there.

And her face tells me she's heard everything.

I get what my mother has been saying now. What it means to show I have heart. Zoey.

*She's* my heart.

I'm a book of clichés in love with her. Zoey showed me I have a heart.

But the thing I didn't know was that they shatter.

Because I might just have gone and destroyed my heart.

Zoey holds everything.

I get to my feet.

"Zoey?"

# Chapter Thirty

## ZOEY

Magnus looks at me like I'm his world, like I hold his happiness. And the woman he told me was his mother stands there, smiling like she's just pulled off the match of the century.

He scowls at her. "Mother."

"I'm leaving." She steps toward me and touches my arm. "Welcome to the family, I hope."

I stare at her as she leaves and play over everything I heard. "Was I a game, Magnus?"

"You were never a game." He walks slowly halfway across the room and stops. "Not like that."

"She said I won you something?"

I breathe out. Wait.

"My dead father decided to test us all for the family heirloom jewels." He shrugs. "My brother had to fall in love and I had to show I had heart."

I squeeze shut my eyes. "By getting me to love you? And you saving my business?"

"What? No. I set up a bunch of foundations and charities. I have them here."

He goes to the desk and I follow, I don't know why. I'm weak. I love him. He hands me another folder and I take it and flip through, pausing on the page labeled Helena Smith Foundation. Page after page of things he's set up are there. Small and big and only one thing is named after his family name. My hands tremble as I smooth my fingers back on that page named after my grandmother.

"It's a safe place for kids and young people, to go and read or hang out and do homework, to exchange books. Just something I figured would be helpful in different communities. Not a library, even though so many are closing down or becoming privatized, but a place where kids can feel safe and just be with an emphasis on books." He wipes a hand over the back of his neck.

"What you heard," he says, "was my mother pointing out the real heart I showed was you. Falling for you. She's an annoying woman. A pain in my ass. And very astute."

"So what am I meant to do? Just forgive you?"

"You know, I went to you earlier today with the plan to do that. I could have just sent you everything. Made it formal and soulless. But I didn't."

"You're selfish."

"Yeah."

I nod, a spark of hope blooming inside me. "I could live with selfish."

"Thing is, I wanted to learn about who was in my way and then I met you and you got in my heart. I did all that for you. That wasn't selfish. That cost me a lot of money. And will. I can afford it, but I don't waste money for anyone. Except you. Because I love you."

Suddenly he frowns. "Wait. Did you say you loved me?"

"Did I say that?"

"Yes, you wanted to know if I'd made you fall in love with me to get what I wanted."

I suck in a breath. "Magnus, you manipulated me. You planned to con me. You wanted to take my place from me."

"Yes. And I fell in love with you instead."

"Do you think I should forgive you?"

A look of pain crosses his beautiful face. "No. Not at all. But if you do, I'll spend my life winning you over, proving my love, making myself worthy of you. I've never been in love before, so I'm not good at it. All I know is you're in my mind first thing in the morning and last thing at night." He stops. "Fuck, I sound like a terrible love song."

"I don't mind."

"You don't?"

"I love you, too. I'm not good at holding grudges, Magnus. And I think you were you once you stopped the doormat nice guy routine early on."

He comes up to me, a half smile on his face. "Zoey. Are you saying I have a chance?"

"You shouldn't."

"I know."

"You should be made to suffer."

"I already am." He touches me, traces along my cheek, and it's pure magic.

"You don't play fair."

"I know. It's why they call me Asshole Supreme."

I start laughing, I can't help it. And then I stop because he closes the gap between us and pulls out the big guns.

He kisses me.

It's soft and sweet and tender and slow. There's passion and love and longing and regret. And hope.

The kiss contains a bright and shining future if I'm brave enough, stupid enough, reckless enough to take it.

And I do. I slide my arms about him and deepen the kiss and finally when it's over he smiles down at me, his dimple flashing and making me weak all over.

"I love you, Zoey," he says, running his thumb along my lip. "You've ruined me. You got me eating those cookies you make. Already you have the devotion of my PA. That's who I gave the cookies and cake to when you sent them home for Amelia. And also my mother, who ate the ones I left in here. I'm not really into sugar, or I wasn't, but you make magic happen."

"In my cookies and cakes?"

He grins. "Those, yes, but I meant you. You're the magic ingredient. You make anything the right kind of sweet, Zoey."

"You don't have to convince me to love you," I say.

Magnus releases me and leans against his desk, letting his gaze move slowly over me. "Actually, I do. I need to win you every day. Because I think you're worth it. I never got the deal about heart. But I do now. And falling in love with you, I can see some things are worth more than money."

My heart swells. "If I asked you to give it all up would you?"

"In a second. I'm not saying we take ourselves to the poorhouse, but yeah, I'd give up my empire for you."

I fan myself with one hand and try to breathe. "You know what? You don't have to do that. Not unless you want. But if you stick to those plans you gave me, you did something better. You saved my neighborhood. Progressed it, sure, but you're giving back. You're giving those who love it a place to live and where they can afford to live."

His cheeks turn darker. "There'll be jobs, too. I did that for you, for them." He picks up two boxes that are on his desk and looks at me. "Why did you come here?"

"Because I love you."

He nods. "I didn't get why my mother gave me this," he says, handing me a black box. "But I think it's for you."

I open it and gasp. It's a beautiful key. "This is meant to represent your heart. Well, the way in, the way to protect it."

"Is it?"

"Look at it."

He laughs softly. "Actually, that sounds just like my mother. I think you're right. My heart needs to be in safe hands, Zoey. And I can't think of better hands than yours."

"You know, I think a key like this works both ways."

"It does?"

I nod. "Stands to reason it works for mine, too."

"I like that." He pushes away from the table. "I think a key that works like that means it's got to be the forever kind. One that comes with a ring. Vows."

Now I really can't breathe. I don't even know how I got here. But the happiness inside me is flying so high it's looping the loop and it feels completely and utterly right. He's an asshole, but he's mine.

Mine.

"And I think," I say, "that you should marry me, like you say. And not just because of that. Thing is, you're new at all this being good thing. I think you need someone around to make sure you don't fall off the wagon and back into your black-hearted ways."

He slides an arm around me. "I like that plan. I do need someone like that. Someone sweet and strong and stubborn who can keep me under control."

I kiss him and it's perfect.

Magnus sighs and leans his forehead against mine a moment. "I don't have a ring. Not yet. But I have the Sinclair earrings, if you'd like them."

He opens the other box and they glint at me. They're delicate gold and rose-colored diamond tear drops. Beautiful, understated, and old. I fall in love with them, too. "I accept."

"I never thought someone else could make me so happy."

"Stick with me," I say. "I've got a lot more to teach you."

"I'd love that." He kisses me again. "I'm so sorry I hurt you, Zoey."

"I could say you can make it up to me the rest of our lives, but you know what?"

"What?"

I take a breath. "I'd rather just spend the rest of our lives loving each other, good times and bad."

"I can live with that."

He kisses me and sets down the earrings and the key, then he picks up an envelope.

"What is it?"

"For my brothers." He opens it and scans it and puts it down. "I've got a feeling Ryder's next. The board of our father's company, our heritage, isn't happy with his shenanigans, and I think there's something else going on. My mother is poking her nose into all this, and..." He kisses me again. "And I don't know why. I have three brothers. I'm telling you this because there are two of them, Ryder and Kingston, who have yet to face whatever's thrown at them for their piece of our inheritance. And if you marry into this family, you're going to be involved whether you like it or not."

"A mystery?" I start to smile.

"A pain in the ass," he says. "But whatever's going on, that's up to them. I've got a wedding to plan." He stops. "We. We have. Unless you changed your mind."

"You're stuck with me, Edward Magnus Sinclair."

"Good, because you're stuck with me. For the rest of our lives."

"Deal."

"I love a good deal. And I love you, Zoey."

This time he kisses me with heat and passion and so much love I know this is a forever thing.

No matter what happened before. We have a future ahead of us and no matter what happens, it's going to be good. Because I'll have Magnus. We made it through this. We can make it through anything.

"I love you too," I say.

*This is the end of Magnus and Zoey's love story.*
*But the two, as well as all the other Sinclair brothers, return.*
*The series continues with the story of Ryder. You can find the series here:*
*US: htttps://www.amazon.com/dp/B0D928VLH1*
UK: https://www.amazon.co.uk/dp/B0D928VLH1

# Afterword

Dear reader,

I really hope you enjoyed this story. If so, I would appreciate a short review on Amazon.

As an indie author, I don't have the resources of a major publisher, so this is the way you would support me the most.

# My free romance novel

Would you like to read my free enemies-to-lovers-romance "Date with Hate"?

Then, click here and subscribe and get your free copy instantly into your inbox:

https://sendfox.com/rebeccabaker

Printed in Great Britain
by Amazon